D0117591

DOUGLAS ADAMS

STARSHIP TITANIC

THE OFFICIAL STRATEGY GUIDE

by

Neil Richards

THREE RIVERS PRESS
NEW YORK

Published by Three Rivers Press, a division of Crown Publishers, Inc.,
201 East 50th Street, New York, New York 10022. Member of the Crown Publishing Group.

Originally published by Pan Books,
an imprint of Macmillan Publishers Ltd., in 1998

Random House, Inc. New York, Toronto, London, Sydney, Auckland
www.randomhouse.com

THREE RIVERS PRESS and colophon are trademarks of Crown Publishers, Inc.

Printed in the United States of America

Design by Eddie Poulton

Library of Congress Cataloging-in-Publication Data is available upon request.

ISBN 0-609-80147-3

10 9 8 7 6 5 4 3 2

Contents

S
T
R
A
T
E
G
Y

G
U
I
D
E

Acknowledgments

I would like to thank: Robbie, Douglas and Ted for giving me the opportunity of working on both the Game and the Guide; the whole ST Team for their help with the book in spite of tough deadlines; John and Darren at Voodoo for the extra help with the renders; Eddie Poulton for being patient; Flic Wooldridge for transcribing the interviews; and Annabel, Sam and Joseph for keeping me going...

Neil Richards
March 1998

Foreword

What's going on here? I'm not writing a foreword! I'm a parrot not a foreword writer! I'm not some Ash-Throated Flycatcher you can get to write some bleeding foreword! You want a foreword you go and ask a Band-Rumped Storm-Petrel! You go and ask an Atlantic Puffin. They'll knock off a foreword for you, an Atlantic Puffin will, for just half a sardine. Give 'em a whole sardine and they'll bung you out a couple of prefaces and a whole slew of appendices and a bloody bibliography! But not me, buster, if I can call you buster, you've got the wrong avian!

I'm a parrot, you hear, a parrot! I don't do this stuff! You go and consult any reputable textbook on parrot behaviour and see where it says anything about the composition of forewords for game manuals! It's not what we do! We have our pride! We're not like those Black-Faced Grassquit Hacks! We're not a load of Hudsonian Godwit Literary Sluts!

Alright, give us a nut and I'll do it.

A. Parrot

Also by Douglas Adams

Introduction by Douglas Adams

I'm not allowed into the programmers' room any more. We are about two days from final delivery of the game. They are chasing down the very last of the bugs, making sure that the cursors all point the right way, and that there are no hitherto unnoticed glitches in the control interface. So my habit of wandering in and saying, "Hey, here's a great idea, why don't we put in a bit where...?" is beginning to get to them. That and the long nights they've all spent sleeping on couches or floors around the office, living off coffee, cold pizza and crumbs of encouragement from people like me saying "Do you think the parrot might look better in green?" They're all brilliant heroes, I salute them, and I'm not at all surprised they don't want to see me this week.

A lot of people have been saying to me, with worried, searching looks, "How come the CD-ROM is six months late?" The answer is very simple. It's because it's a bloody CD-ROM, that's why. All CD-ROMs are six months late. At least. It's an immutable law of the universe. The only surprising thing about ours being late is that we were surprised by it. We had no idea – well, certainly I had no idea – of the scale of the enterprise we were undertaking.

Probably the biggest task, certainly the biggest leap into the unknown, was handling the language interaction. Nothing on this scale had ever been attempted in a computer game before. In fact, everybody whose advice we sought said we couldn't do it and would be mad to even attempt it. A good challenge. Clearly the task was beyond the scope of any one person and we recruited a small team of dialogue writers to work with me, including Neil Richards and Michael Bywater. Michael is an old friend who had already worked with me sketching out the structure of the game. Neil knew little about computers and was therefore easily fooled into taking on the task of managing and editing the dialogue, a job that dominated his life for the next year. It was huge.

We started very simply, sketching out some of the things that we imagined a player might think of saying to the characters and what the characters should say in response. We brought in actors to record the lines, programmed them into the game and tested it to see how it worked. It was pathetic. For every input line we had thought of there were ninety-nine we hadn't. So we started on a second, much, much deeper and longer set of scripts to cover what we had overlooked, and got the actors in again, this time to record reams and reams of sentences, phrases, words, numbers, names, burps, sneezes and names of chicken recipes. This all got coded into the game, and again it wasn't remotely enough. The problem was increasing like a fractal, and was rendered almost impossibly more complicated by the fact that I had recklessly decided early on that each of the Bots would have a series of different moods and behaviours, each of which had to be covered for any given situation. So for instance, the BarBot might be in charming mood or a belligerent mood, might be telling the truth or lying, and might be more or less able to come to the point quickly. Or any combination of any of the above. This was a hideous, hideous problem. Especially for Neil who did most of the work on the BarBot and became a haggard, hunted creature as we went through this write, record, test, and rewrite iteration time after time over the course of a year.

We ended up with over sixteen hours of little snippets of dialogue. Over ten thousand lines. YOU WILL NOT GET BORED TALKING TO THESE ROBOTS. Some people who have tried the game have asked if this is an exercise in artificial intelligence. No. Not even remotely. Just as when a stage magician saws his assistant in half and then joins her together again it isn't an exercise in medical science. It's a trick, an illusion, albeit a highly complex and sophisticated one. When you're playing Starship Titanic the computer doesn't "understand" anything. It just assesses the players' input according to a simple set of rules and then chooses an appropriate output. Watch any Presidential debate and you'll get the idea. Having gone this far though, it seems a pity that we didn't just go all out for trying to achieve artificial intelligence while we were about it. Hell, there's a good couple of days before we finally freeze the code, maybe I'll just pop along to the programmers' room and see if they're up for it.

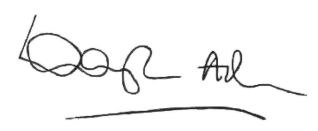

How to Use This Book

There's nothing worse than opening a Strategy Guide at the wrong page and finding the solution to a puzzle that hasn't even begun to puzzle you yet.

So how do you avoid that happening here? For a start, DON'T READ the chapter called SOLUTIONS unless you're hopelessly, incurably, irrevocably STUCK. Because the SOLUTIONS chapter doesn't muck about. Oh no. You want solutions – that's what you get. There's no wishy-washy "Try this" or "Try that": just plain 'Do this, click on that, drag it over and now get on with the next one...'

If you have to use the SOLUTIONS chapter then you should use the mini-index on page 107. That way you won't stumble across the solution to another puzzle by mistake.

The HINTS chapter on the other hand is essentially a walk-through of the game. You'll get suggestions, possible dialogue routes, descriptions of the important objects in the rooms (just in case you miss something) and, of course, hints...

The chapter called THE BUGLE gives you back-story and clues about the Starship Titanic, her crew and creators, all of which might help you solve the mysteries of the ship. Then again it might not.

Getting Technical

Starship Titanic is big. Really big. You might think Microsoft Encarta is big, but that's peanuts compared to Starship Titanic. It comes on more than one CD-ROM, for a start. The more intelligent readers will have noticed that I didn't say exactly how many CDs it comes on. The less intelligent readers will have stopped reading by now because their lips are tired.

I did not mention how many CDs there are, because I'm not entirely sure yet. This is because I am writing this before Starship Titanic has been completely finished. So I could tell you a number, but that number might go down or up, depending on how well I've budgeted for our cleverness or stupidity. For now, just assume we're really clever. It saves a whole bunch of time. In fact, due to the ridiculous lead times publishers need, this is being written before Starship Titanic has even been started. Honestly — my current job is working as a Windows applications programmer — I haven't even joined The Digital Village, nor have I even heard of it yet. The first episode of the Hitchhiker radio series has just been broadcast for the first time. This enormous lead time is required by publishers, because when I e-mail this copy to Neil, he will then e-mail it to the publishers, who will print it out on a daisy- wheel printer, and give it to their copy "boy", Jebediah, who will then "run" down the Oxford Road until he gets to the print-ing press. Well, I say printing press. Two guys in a field with some rocks and chisels, if you want the facts.

But I digress. It's something I do. As my silver-haired old grandmother used to say, "Get to the point before I shoot you like a dog in the street." And she always told me Goldie went to stay on someone's farm. Ha. The main symptom of Starship Titanic com-ing on more than one CD is that you will, as the player of this spectacular game, be prompted to change CDs periodically. When you insert a CD, spare a thought for us, the technical team, who worked hard to make sure this happens as little as possible while you play the game. It was a non-stop workarama — at one stage, Sean even typed in some source code. Rik and Adam frequently interrupted their top-level Carmageddon briefings to bring this elegant game to you. On many occasions Emma "Code Spice" Westecott would stop scaring the life out of the artists and click a few mouse buttons. Hell, some days I even came into work before eleven-thirty.

So you know how we struggled to ease your pain. If we save you some inconve-nience as a result, it makes our day. Of course, you might say that the frequent articles in magazines and newspapers complaining about the failure of "geeks" and "nerds" to make computers easier to use for "normal" people would be reward enough. But somehow, uninformed bigots are just not enough for us – we need to make life easier for you, the real people. The people with tired lips. So we have. Trust me – I'm not a real programmer. (Don't worry – it's another joke for the geeks.)

Oh yes. The technical stuff. Assuming you have opposable thumbs, here are some tips for handling those pesky CD-ROMs:

Put them in with the printing on the uppermost surface – they work better like that.

Take them out of the case first. (Trust me, this has an even bigger effect than the whole right-way-up thing.)

Do not, as I was gravely warned by the instructions of a game I bought recently, put CDs into your drive that have been "mended with glue". Important safety tip, guys.

Tim Browse
Technical Lead
Starship Titanic Project
March 1998

TITANIC TRAGEDY SPECIAL EDITION

LOST!

Last confirmed sighting
of Starship Titanic

THE BLERONTIN BUGLE — TITANIC TRAGEDY SPECIAL EDITION

ON OTHER PAGES

⌁⌁⌁⌁⌁ *"We will be Blamed"* warns the Yeller. Yassaccans fear reprisals.

⌁⌁⌁⌁⌁ SMEF – Spontaneous Massive Existence Failure. *"Have we gone too far?"* asks our Hair and Beauty Correspondent.

⌁⌁⌁⌁⌁ Nib matches may be postponed. Blerontin Girls stranded in Vastan. *"Execution of Vastan Chiefs of Staff just a precaution"* says team coach Clem Grunt.

⌁⌁⌁⌁⌁ Full two-page recipe for Leovinus's Award-Winning Canape.

⌁⌁⌁⌁⌁ Fortillian O'Perfluous (whose personality was on board) mixes a Commemorative Cocktail and talks about the tragedy.

⌁⌁⌁⌁⌁ *"We knew it would end in tears"* – The Wives of The Missing speak out from their Secret Mountain Hideaway.

⌁⌁⌁⌁⌁ *"InterGalactic Travel still safer than eating mints"* says Leader of Blerontin Tourist Fraternity.

⌁⌁⌁⌁⌁ The Gat of Blerontis promises: *"Something will be done. By someone. Somewhere."*

⌁⌁⌁⌁⌁ Hernandez Terpsicoid on that famous pink sheeting: *"Forget the Titanic – that was the real disaster!"*

ALSO: Nasal Hair – is it making a Comeback?

LEOVINUS FEARED PERISHED.

◆

The loss of Leovinus, feared perished on the ill-fated Titanic, has cast a shadow not just across Blerontin but deep into the known Galaxy. This extraordinary man, at ease both with pastry-cutter and cybo-dynamic lance, has blazed a trail of invention across our lives for many decades.

Leovinus was destined for greatness. His father was the legendary soprazzo Zoltan B. Link (later to become the Astronomer Laureate), his mother the renowned Hat Designer Xorastes Taul. Leovinus's birth, in a cave high in the mountain ranges of Talabok during the Eleventh Revolutionary War, is the stuff of legend. Both his parents were soldiers in the 8th Operatic Commando during the Ten Year Siege of Kalaboosh, and Leovinus was to spend his formative years at their side. At the age of 4 he had twice been decorated for valour: his invention, at the age of 8, of the Seamless Bomb Lobber, turned the tide of the war. When the victorious armies entered Blerontis Leovinus was placed at their helm to receive the City's surrender.

Brilliant in war, the young Leovinus was soon to shine in peace. Enrolled as a Platinum Member of the Blerontis Academy of Very Difficult Things he soon took degrees in astrophysics, molecular biology, geophysics, painting, sculpture, mechanical design, physics, anatomy, music, poetry, crystallography, thermodynamics, weaponry, electromagnetism and philosophy. Unbeknownst to his fellow students he also taught himself canape arrangement – his breathtaking

debut at the All-Blerontis Singles in '43 and his dazzling victory in the Finals in straight trays led immediately to a place in the National team and the first of many Limpiad Gold Medals. His similar domination of the Hopping Competition was to lead to the accumulation of ten Land Speed Records in all.

The years immediately following his graduation were to be disappointing ones however. In his autobiography *An Ordinary Life Lived Not Once But Twiceover is The Same As A Single Life Lived Quite Slowly* he

THE BLERONTIN BUGLE — TITANIC TRAGEDY SPECIAL EDITION

draws a veil over some of the darker events. Certainly he lost his way – there are rumours of experiments with hot gasses and yodelling. He was twice arrested for carrying flowers. His involvement with the Revolutionary Shoe cannot be denied. Finally, on advice from the Gat himself, Leovinus's parents sent him to the Architectural Monastery of Reborzo for a period of reflection. There the great Monsignor Zoot Bilgewater took him under his wing and showed him – Architecture.

What schoolboy now cannot recite the list of Towering Achievements which were to stem from that inspired journey to Reborzo: the great North-South Bridge that links our two polar caps; the Pandax Building with its inter-changeable rooms; the Collapsible Galaxy; the Disposable Shopping Planets; the astonishing Twirly Wirly City with its single concentric road; our Third Sun that now shines above us with its famous On-Off Switch.

Leovinus was truly prodigious, never tiring of new projects, always challenging, forever winning awards. The list of his inventions is staggering: Long-Distance Hair Removal; Cars; the Ionic Hedge-Trimmer; the Cyber-Optic Trouser Press; BrainFarming; Re-usable Electricity; the Reversible Sausage; de-aging Cream. The list is endless. The last and most incredible invention of the great Leovinus's genius however was the propulsion system for the Starship Titanic – the vastest source of power in the probable universe – a captive Black Hole. Using the tried and tested Higgs Shell this should have been his greatest triumph, his final gift to a grateful Blerontis. We shall never know quite why – or indeed if – it failed. Quite probably only a mind

such as Leovinus could tell us. And in truth, there shall never be such a mind again.

BLERONTIN STOCK EXCHANGE.

◆

DULL ON THE LOSS OF THE TITANIC

The Stock Market has today been quieter than for some little time, partly no doubt owing to the gloom cast over the business world by the Titanic Disaster. The tendency has been reactionary and the majority of the active stocks show losses on the day.

The chief among these are: Higgs Engineering three and one eighth, Galactic Centrals and Star Trust Common one and one quarter, Yassacan Polish two, Vastan Preferreds one and seven eighths, SnorkBarrels seven eighths. StarStruct Inc and Starlight Travel withdrawn from trading.

On the Ancillary Comestibles and Unscheduled Assets Market, Fish Paste was unchanged. Lard was badly hit. Frog Importations have been suspended.

SOME NOTABLE VICTIMS.

MR. A. G. BROBOSTIGON.

Antar Galoot Brobostigon whose redoubtable managerial career has been abruptly closed by the loss of the Titanic was a stalwart of the Blerontinian commercial world.

THE BLERONTIN BUGLE — TITANIC TRAGEDY SPECIAL EDITION

Born the twenty-ninth son of the heretical Bishop of Ab, Antar was brought up in his father's absence by his uncle, a chicken-farmer who sadly perished in a husbandry accident when Antar was only eight. Antar inherited the farm and his commercial instincts were soon in evidence: at the age of fourteen he created the first Lend-Lease Poultry Droppings Franchise. The sale of this five years later financed his passage through the Santa Quaraltima School of Usury and Small Book-Keeping. "Quazzers" was the making of Brobostigon: he graduated Top Chap of his year and was made Student With Very Big Hat. After a year's Hardening, he joined InterGal as a junior manager in the prestigious Lethal Injections Department.

Fate was now to play its well-manicured hand in Brobostigon's career: the Great War Of Vastan helped him to triple turnover without risking capital and he soon earned himself a reputation as a "safe pair of hands". Not that he was without a certain impish humour: as the Conflict neared its end Brobostigon caused much hilarity amongst his colleagues with a nightly Cloud-Light Display showing InterGal's profits comically sparring with the latest casualty figures.

When InterGal decided to set up its Very Nasty Weapons Division, Antar was chosen to head it. He was in his element and over the next few years earned the fear and respect of all his employees. Never one to be chained to a desk, he would often be seen down in the testing beds in shirtsleeves and robe firing off experimental rounds at the prisoner volunteers from the nearby divorce courts. It was there that he met and fell in love with

his wife-to-be Crossa. Their lavish honeymoon in the Field Wounds Centre on Izioma was the envy of many. On their return Crossa worked alongside Antar for many years as he moved up the ranks at InterGal, initially with the Very Small and Still Quite Noisy Ships Division before finally accepting the challenge of The Department of Extremely Grand Liners.

Sadly, a disastrous accident whilst Antar and Crossa were away on vacation led to the closure of InterGal's entire shipbuilding facilities and Antar was forced to retire briefly from employment. Always reluctant to talk of this episode in his life he would briskly remind the casual observer that he had been completely exonerated in the ensuing public enquiry.

After devoting the next five years to the construction of his own impressive 20 bedroom ocean-facing villa, Antar returned to the ship-building industry with the ill-fated position of project manager on the Titanic. It is a tribute to his skills that there have been only two hundred fatalities under his stewardship, and less than fifty of these have been accidental. His loss will be deeply felt not just in the weapons and shipping industries but also by the Santa Quaraltima Boy Choristers' Association of which he was an enthusiastic supporter.

Mr Brobostigon is survived by his wife Crossa and one Hermaphrodite, Lorn.

MR. D. SCRALIONTIS.

Droot Scraliontis came from a long line of Accountants. Born

unusually on Chitterling Day he benefited throughout his life from the extra tax concessions offered by the Chitterling Foundation and accepted their offer of a scholarship to Coin College. Having entered the service of the Penitential Assurance Co in '58 he rapidly rose to a position of prominence. The highest of all actuarial honours was bestowed upon him in '74 viz the election to the Presidential Chair for the customary term of two years. He went into private practice in '77. An avid collector of sand, he was a founder member of the Sand Society and lectured throughout the galaxy.

Mr Scraliontis is survived by his wife Wyde. He had three Worbs, which will be put down.

THE BLERONTIN BUGLE — TITANIC TRAGEDY SPECIAL EDITION

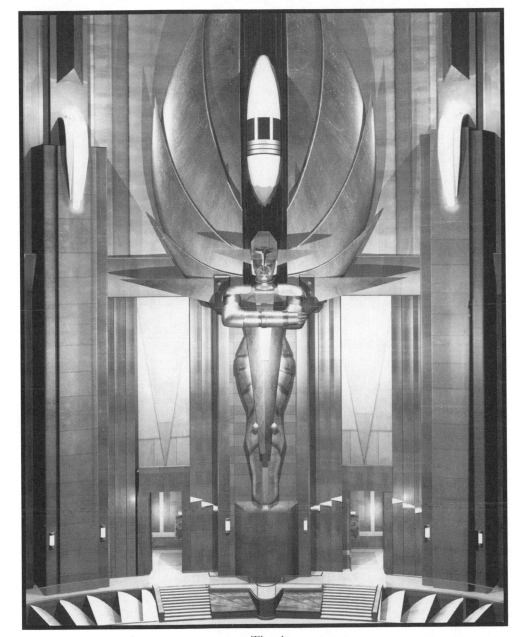

Titania

Remote Thingummy

THE PET

The PET is your interface with the Starship Titanic.
It can be used in many different ways on board the ship:
to talk to the Bots, to call a lift, to turn on a TV or even to
re-arrange the furniture. It has five distinct modes:
Chat-O-Mat; Personal Baggage; Remote Thingummy;
Designer Room Numbers; and Real Life.

The PET comes in three different shiny finishes depending
upon what class you are. On the Starship Titanic of course.

Each mode is represented by an icon on the right hand side. Click on the appropriate icon with the cursor to select a mode or to change modes. Whichever mode you are in – the relevant icon is highlighted. In some situations the PET mode will change automatically when there has been an important game event: for example, if you are upgraded it will change from Chat-O-Mat to Designer Room Number mode to show you your new room number, even though you are talking to the DeskBot.

Chat-O-Mat

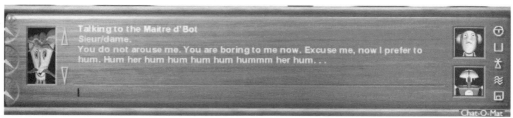

Use this mode to talk to the Bots. The box on the left hand side of the PET shows which Bot you are currently talking to. You can summon Bots in most rooms: the boxes on the right hand side show which Bots are available. To summon a Bot click on its image. To review a conversation, use the scroll arrows.

Personal Baggage

This is a kind of inventory. It shows you what game objects you have already picked up. If you come across an object that you want to put in your PET, simply click on it and drag it into an empty box. (In fact your PET will even accept objects if you're not in Personal Baggage mode.) You can also drag items out of the PET – to put them in the Succ-U-Bus tray or give to a Bot, for example. As your Personal Baggage fills up you may find it necessary to scroll using the arrows to reveal new empty boxes.

Remote Thingummy

TV (SGT Stateroom)

Lift

Lights

Succ-U-Bus

Use this mode to control various objects on board the ship (the Elevator, Pellerator, TV, Succ-U-Bus, for example). Whenever there is a controllable object in a room it will always appear in one of the boxes of Remote Thingummy mode. Just select the icon of the item you wish to control and the appropriate buttons will appear on the right hand side of the PET.

Most of the objects which you control in Remote Thingummy mode are simple to operate. The Starfield is more complex, however:

Navigation Helmet

Starfield Operation

Designer Room Numbers

Every room on the ST has a unique chevron identifier which you will see on walls etc. The PET always displays in the right hand box the chevron representing the room in which you are currently standing. You can create a library of rooms you have visited: to do this, each time you enter a room, drag the icon from the right-hand box into an empty box. These chevrons can be used to tell the Succ-U-Bus the destination for any object you are sending: simply drag the chevron onto the activated Succ-U-Bus then go to Remote Thingummy mode and tell him what to do. To copy a chevron or create a new one, you can edit the chevron in the right-hand box using your cursor with the SHIFT key depressed.

Real Life

Use this mode when you want to return to Reality.

Save

Click on this to save up to six different games. Games can be numbered or named according to your preference.

Load

Click on this to reveal your saved games. Just click to select then press return or hit the load button.

Volume

Click on this to set the volume levels of the game. The different controls affect general volume, character volume, room volume etc.

THE BOTS

"In the Titanic universe, donating your personality
(i.e. getting your brain scanned for use in a robot) is like
being a blood-donor in America — something you do for a
bit of cash. The 'better' your personality the more money
you get for it.   What happens to a mind that has been
scanned and stored in software? It has to work its way up
the ranks. All the minds on Starship Titanic are now in
pretty prestigious jobs but they've had to work their way
up through being the onboard intelligences in toasters,
speak-your-weight machines, on-screen help, VCRs, etc."

Douglas Adams

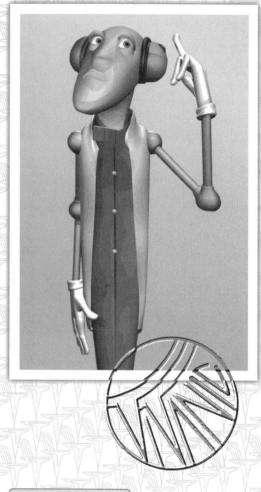

IDENTIFICATION CARD & SERVICE RECORD

Issued by The Blerontin Council of Transport & Ethics

Name:
Edmund Lucy Fentible

Type:
DoorBot

Class:
Premier (Hons)

Reg. no:
XL3TL 656 9835

No. of former keepers:
14

Model:
Witherskip Humbler

Comments:
Nav. – Central Areas only

Maintenance:

Dejection infection located and debugged. Jps 14.2.0989

Woe display corrected. Memory reinstalled. Jps 66.3.0989

Fatal memory collapse. Optimism re-scaled. Jps 67.3. 0989

Head cleaned and buffed. K. Natwakket. 70/3/0989

registered to: **Star-Struck Inc.**

We take pride in our Bots. Should you be disappointed in any way with this Bot's
appearance or behaviour do not hesitate, *Feel* disappointed.

ETHER CARTE™

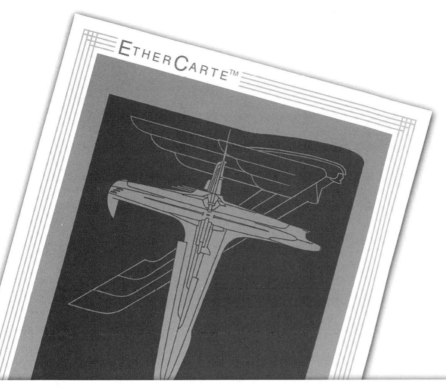

ETHER CARTE™

> ...... Edwina

> ...... Ahoy from deep space! You always
said you'd get me up here one day - well
three cheers for personality transfers.
> ...... So far all gone swimmingly although
departure from Blerontin trifle swift for my
tastes. Ship not quite as ship-shape as
had been led to expect. Behaviour of some
of crew leaves much to be desired. All
going to end in tears.

> ....Funny. Can't seem to remember who
you are anymore.
> ...... Where's the sense in it all...

> ...... Edmund

<END>

DOORBOT

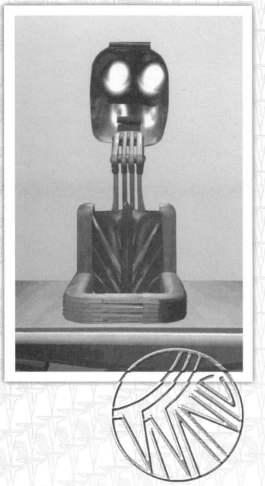

IDENTIFICATION CARD & SERVICE RECORD

Issued by The Blerontin Council of Transport & Ethics

Name:

Marsinta Drewbish

Type:

DeskBot

Class:

Superior

Reg. no:

HKE911 2234

No. of former keepers:

1

Model:

Indefatigable (auto)

Comments:

Nav. restriction – Embarkation Lobby

Maintenance:

Discretion Regulator re-installed. H.G. 15.3.0989

Lig-Buster 1.8 loaded. Jps 66.3.0989

Put-Em-Down 2 loaded. Jps 67.3. 0989

Upgrade-Ratifier checked. Jps 69.3.0989

Bell shined. Norb. 70/3/0989

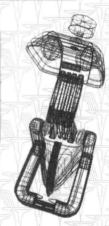

registered to: **Star-Struct Inc.**

We take pride in our Bots. Should you be disappointed in any way with this Bot's appearance or behaviour do not hesitate. *Feel* disappointed.

ETHER CARTE™

> ...... Papa

> ...... I will not be moved on the block-share issue and it is unfair of you to use grandfather's will to try and persuade me. (You conveniently forget clause 23a which effectively anticipates and negates the course of action you seem determined to follow.) If you persist in this matter I shall have no alternative but to bring it to a vote at the next family meeting.

> ......Give my love to Hettie.

> ...... The voyage is proving uneventful. Do not forget to water the philospanglias by the boat house. If any Worbs are leaving droppings there, have them destroyed.

> ...... In haste,

> ...... Marsinta.

<END>

DESKBUT

IDENTIFICATION CARD & SERVICE RECORD

Issued by The Blerontin Council of Transport & Ethics

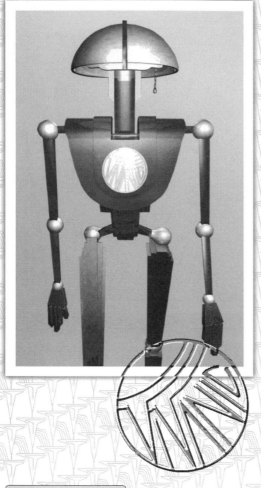

Name:
Krage Koyotoaal IV

Type:
BellBot

Class:
Third

Reg. no:
XT7X1LNV 878 2209

No. of former keepers:
87

Model:
Discontinued

Comments:
Nav. – Most Areas

Maintenance:

Corrupted Assistance Drive replaced. Jps 102.3.0989

Thru-Pass upgraded. Jps 102.3.0989

Default humour settings checked. Hg. 66.3.0989

New bulb fitted. Ken Natwakket. 70/3/0989

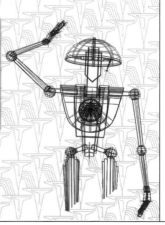

registered to: **Star-Struct Inc.**

We take pride in our Bots. Should you be disappointed in any way with this Bot's appearance or behaviour do not hesitate. *Feel* disappointed.

ETHERCARTE™

ETHERCARTE™

> ...... Hi guys

> ...... Whew what a trip!

> ...... Two hours after take-off we got hit
in a big way by a fleet of Yassacan barge-
busters. Took a lot of collateral but yours
truly seized command and after a fire-fight
that makes the siege of Vastan look like a
fish-paste convention we triumphed and
brought peace again to this troubled
corner of the galaxy.

> ...... Ha! Just kidding. Slept through take-
off. Looking forward to payday.

> ......Krage

"If It's Heading For The Beach I'll Ride It"

<END>

© Larry's Novelty Cards, Small Mail Bierontis

BELLBOT

IDENTIFICATION CARD & SERVICE RECORD

Issued by The Blerontin Council of Transport & Ethics

Name:
G. Nobbington-Froat

Type:
LiftBot

Class:
Other

Reg. no:
BGL 340 419 2883

No. of former keepers:
835

Model:
Limb-Lop

Comments:
Nav. restriction – Elevators

Maintenance:

PTSD refreshed. Jps 14.3.0989

Syphohrea directory updated. Jps 66.3.0989

Arm lubed. Woodbine changed. R. Sneb 70/3/0989

registered to: **Star-Struct Inc.**

We take pride in our Bots. Should you be disappointed in any way with this Bot's appearance or behaviour do not hesitate. *Feel* disappointed.

ETHER CARTE™

> ...... Major-General Lithium Hatravers, Master of the Golden Gourd.

> ...... Well it's a rum do and no mistake. If this reaches you I'll have been through something nigh on diabolical and come out the other side. If it doesn't then I'll have caught one gift-wrapped as Archy used to say.

> ...... With my lungs it didn't ought to be me what's got to work this out, but I'll tell you now there's been some jiggery pokery on board this boat and no mistake.

> ...... Mum's the word for now but line 'em up for me at the Legion bar and we'll read the entrails together when I'm back in Blaggerty eh?

> ...... Nobbie.

<END>

LIFTBOT

IDENTIFICATION CARD & SERVICE RECORD

Issued by The Blerontin Council of Transport & Ethics

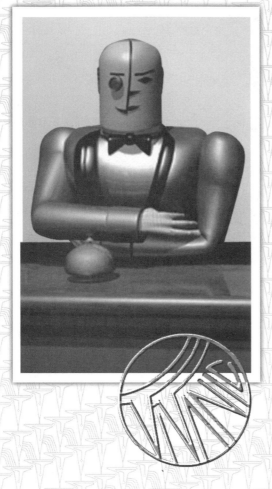

Name:

Fortillian Bantoburn O'Perfluous

Type:

BarBot

Class:

First (probationary)

Reg. no:

VF7XBER 000 2299

No. of former keepers:

5

Model:

Blargh Ironymaster 2.1

Comments:

Nav. restriction – Bar, First Class.

Maintenance:

Charm re-balanced, Exaggerator uninstalled. Jps 14.3.0989
Digression Engine sympathised. Jps 66.3.0989
New Nib Directory loaded. Jps 67.3.0989
Honesty settings re-configured. Jps 69.3.0989
Oiled and gutted. Jokes changed. K. Natwakket. 70/3/0989

registered to: **Star-Struct Inc.**

We take pride in our Bots. Should you be disappointed in any way with this Bot's appearance or behaviour do not hesitate. *Feel* disappointed.

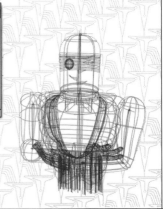

ETHERCARTE™

ETHERCARTE™

> ...... Boys

> ...... You tell Rafferty I'll be home soon to take up his offer. Forget that tip he calls a bar - you'll be drinking in Bantoburn's from now on and it won't just be pints of Slug, oh no, I've learnt a thing or two on this trip.

> ...... My god but Rafferty's a mean squint-eyed fish of a fellow now I think of him.

> ...... Funny - I've been having some rare old mood swings since we left Blerontin...but what the hell.

> ...... To the greater glory of gullets everywhere!!!

> ...... Fortillian.

<END>

BARBOT

IDENTIFICATION CARD & SERVICE RECORD

Issued by The Blerontin Council of Transport & Ethics

Name:
D'Astragar (D'Astragaaar) D'Astragar

Type:
Maitre d'Bot

Class:
Exclusif

Reg. no:
LKHF 354 0298

No. of former keepers:
5

Model:
Galloid Marque 1

Comments:
Nav. restriction – First Class Restaurant

Maintenance:

Servility settings re-tuned. Jps 14.3.0989

Irascibility levels checked. Jps 66.3.0989

Accent upgraded. Jps 67.3.0989

Hollandaise Sauce stain identified & removed from fly. R. Sneb. 70/3/0989

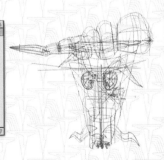

registered to: **Star-Struct Inc.**

We take pride in our Bots. Should you be disappointed in any way with this Bot's appearance or behaviour do not hesitate. *Feel* disappointed.

ETHERCARTE™

> ...... Members of the Academy

> ...... I report to you what I have seen already. Certainly the kitchens are unimpeachable. I have no qualms and there is required security around the frog enclosures.

> ...... As feared however, my station has been positioned in the low-visibility areas in COMPLETE contradiction of the agreement reached at the Interim Comestibles Committee. This big flouting

can only benefit the wine waiters, and I have some small horror at the outcome. If need be, I am prepared for a fight and I tell you I will fight.

> ...... With continued regard for your support,

> ...... I remain,

> ...... D'Astragaaar.

<END>

MAÎTRE D'BOT

IDENTIFICATION CARD & SERVICE RECORD

Issued by The Blerontin Council of Transport & Ethics

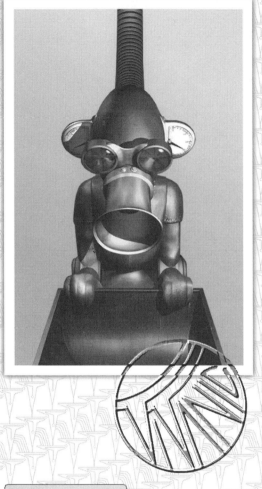

Name:

Shorbert Sweet

Type:

Succ-U-Bus

Class:

N/A

Reg. no:

GT55SR 0 9585

No. of former keepers:

8987787

Model:

Gut-Buster 2

Comments:

Nav. restriction – All Areas

Maintenance:

Fowling tubes re-grouted. Don Lout 14.3.0989

Bitter sump scoured. Don Lout 15.3.0989

Stank-drains hygenated. Don Lout 16.3.0989

New valve inserted in Fiddly Spigot. Pullijit Lout 17.3.0989

MeadowLark Odor-Envelope to all First Class Stations.

Nicely polished. K. Natwakket. 70/3/0989

registered to: **Star-Struct Inc.**

We take pride in our Bots. Should you be disappointed in any way with this Bot's appearance or behaviour do not hesitate. *Feel* disappointed.

ETHER CARTE™

ETHER CARTE™

> ...... Dear Fleb

> ...... It's no life this.
> ...... I'll bring you back some
booze.

> ...... Shorbert

<END>

SUCC-U BUS

I'm a Parrot.
Anybody tells you I'm a Macaw, spit at them!

I'm a Parrot!

You think I'm some kind of **Barnacle Goose?**

Boreal Chickadee? Common Eider?

Some kind of **Eastern Screech Owl** you can prod?

You think I'm some kind of **Bay-Breasted Warbler?**

Black-Bellied Whistling Duck?

Blossom-Headed Parakeet?

Some kind of **Bohemian Waxwing** to make free with?

You think I'm some kind of **Curve-Billed Thrasher?**

Common Yellow-Throat? Clark's Nutcracker?

Chestnut-Backed Chickadee?

Purple Gallinule? Red-Breasted Sapsucker?

Rough-Legged Hawk?

Pygmy Nuthatch? Piping Plover?

Well I'm not!

I'm a Parrot!

A self-respecting Parrot! Treat me with the respect my position in the catalogue of ornithology betokens!

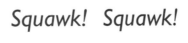

Squawk! Squawk!

I didn't say anything about being a sane Parrot, did I?

Early sketch of Your Lovely Home by Oscar Chichoni.

HINTS

"It's a curious thing about this kind of fantastical computer game: there is both a logic and a great illogic about it. It's an Alice in Wonderland world, where everything makes sense seen from within one frame of reference, but from any other frame of reference is completely insane. It's not because we were determined to be logically illogical or illogically logical but, in the construction of something on this scale there come to be all kinds of little logical worlds that don't necessarily properly fit together – perhaps it doesn't entirely make sense but it's fun so we don't mind!"

Douglas Adams

Getting Started

Starship Titanic isn't a linear game. There are an infinite number of paths through it and most of the puzzles don't have to be solved in a particular order. This chapter is essentially a guided tour. The route I've chosen is one of the more direct but as you become familiar with the ship you'll discover faster ones.

Inevitably some of the puzzles will be revealed in the following pages, but I hope in such a way that you'll still get the chance to figure most of them out for yourself. The puzzles often interconnect: many of the game objects are used more than once but in different ways according to the particular puzzle you are trying to solve.

A few simple rules will speed up your progress.

Firstly, don't forget to read the First Class Inflight Magazine which should have come in your game box – it contains many useful leads. It also contains red herrings – but what do you expect from a game like this?

Follow your primeval upgrade instincts wherever possible. Much of the Starship Titanic is off-limits to 3rd Class Passengers (SGT Class) and you won't solve anything if you can't get into the key rooms.

As you wander around the ship, click on everything – you never know where a useful game object may be hidden in a room.

And finally, don't forget to talk to the Bots – they may often behave irrationally but it's not their fault. They're malfunctioning. Most of the time they want to help...

So, let's get started. I'll assume you've loaded the game, and you are now relaxing in the sitting room of Your Lovely Home. This is a good place to acquaint yourself with the navigation techniques which you will need to move around the Starship Titanic. It's all standard stuff – those of you who play games night and day and no longer have a life will just have to bear with me here while I explain. Using your mouse, move the cursor round the screen. The cursor will change shape or direction whenever it lands on an area that gives you an option of movement. Just left-click and you will move (nav) in the direction your cursor is pointing – this can also be

> ❝ The opening scene of the game has always been known by the team as 'Your Lovely Home' because that is what I jotted down in the script. It wasn't meant to be a formal title, it was just a moment of irony after my first early morning cup of coffee and you know you always like to be a little bit ironic at that point. So I put 'Your Lovely Home' in. I think it was after somebody had been talking to me about 'Hello!' Magazine. ❞
> DOUGLAS ADAMS

Your Lovely Home

up or down. In some cases the cursor will turn into a hand – this indicates there is an object in the vicinity you can grab. Occasionally the cursor turns into a magnifying glass or 'highlights' – this indicates there is either a hidden object or something you can activate. If you want to speed up your movement at any time, simply hold down the shift key as you click – this will cut out the movies which play in between each different view.

Back to Your Lovely Home. This of course is just like your own Lovely Home – but cleaner. Wander round the room, look at the pictures, turn on the TV. You'll find this terribly realistic: repeats on every channel. When you are ready to start the game proper, go to the computer. Click on the CD tray – it will slide out. Grab one of the blank CDs from the table and drop it onto the tray. The CD will run but an error message will appear. Click on the tray, take out the CD and try the other blank. Same problem.

Daytime Television

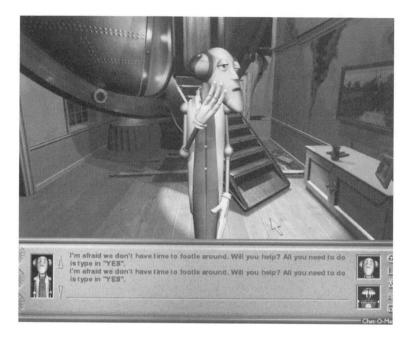

I'm afraid we don't have time to footle around. Will you help? All you need to do is type in "YES".
I'm afraid we don't have time to footle around. Will you help? All you need to do is type in "YES".

LEFT: The DoorBot arrives

RIGHT: The journey begins

You didn't actually have to do that, but a lot of effort went into creating those CDs and it would be a shame if nobody ever played them. Now take the CD with the Starship Titanic logo and drag it onto the tray.

What you're now hearing is the sound of an Intergalactic Liner taking a chunk out of your home insurance policy. This is the Starship Titanic, the Ship That Cannot Possibly Go Wrong, veering out of Hyperspace and into your roof. When the dust has settled a hatch opens and a figure emerges. This is a DoorBot. In fact as there is only one DoorBot on board you ought to know him as *the* DoorBot. His name is Fentible – a gentle soul whose role in normal times would be to welcome guests aboard, answer queries, be civil and of course open doors. At the moment he's down here checking what damage

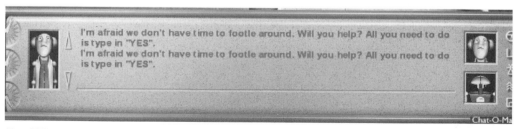

I'm afraid we don't have time to footle around. Will you help? All you need to do is type in "YES".
I'm afraid we don't have time to footle around. Will you help? All you need to do is type in "YES".

Your PET

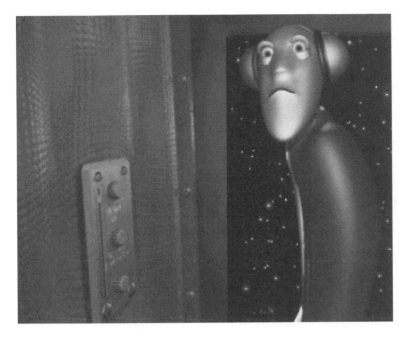

Your Lovely Home has done to the Starship Titanic. He's also about to make you an offer that you cannot refuse: a chance-of-a-lifetime free trip on board the ship.

This opening section of the game is "directed": all you have to do is type YES when Fentible tells you to and listen carefully to what he says. Before you go on board he will give you a PET – a Personal Electronic Thing – which from now until the end of the game will sit at the bottom of your screen.(For details about the PET see page 18.) Fentible will also insist you collect the Picture of the Night Sky from the cupboard on the right. If you don't drag it into your PET he will show you how it's done. As soon as you've agreed to help, Fentible will lead you into the Service Elevator and the steps will close up behind you. Clearly he is not a well Bot – you will have to help him out when he asks you to press the buttons. This memory lapse in the DoorBot is an early clue to the poor fellow's problems. By the way – did you notice that there are three buttons? Remember that – you may need to use this Elevator again.

As the Service Elevator takes you up the side of the ship, you will get a sense of the scale of the Starship Titanic from the view through the window. In the meantime, listen carefully as Fentible explains what's wrong with the ship and what you are going to do to fix it...

After a short while the Service Elevator comes to a halt and you are steered into a large, moonlit room. This is the Embarkation Lobby, a key room on board the Starship Titanic. Fentible disappears to secure the ship for take-off and you are now on your own. You can wander round if you like but you'll soon find you can't do much – all the room exits are sealed. Try the bell on the desk –

A sleeping DeskBot

The Plinth

you might get a muffled voice but that's all. Time to do what Fentible asked – find the plinth and click on the button...

While the Hugely Expensive Opening Credits are rolling, take this opportunity to view the external shape of the ship. Essentially it's a giant T. So far you've only travelled up the outside of the spine of the T so you can see how much more of the Starship Titanic there is to explore.

The Embarkation Lobby

❝ When you finally arrive in The Embarkation Lobby I wanted the sense that it really is very splendid and utterly different from anything one would expect to find in a spaceship. Look at the environments we create in ocean-going ships: why couldn't there be something even more grand than that on spaceships? If this thing actually is a liner – a hotel – then it's got to look like one rather than like a spaceship. ❞

Douglas Adams

When the credits are complete you are returned to the Embarkation Lobby which is now properly lit and functioning. Go over to the desk and try clicking on the bell again. After a second it will open up and another Bot is revealed: the DeskBot. This Check-In-Clerk From Hell goes by the name of Marsinta Drewbish. Be warned: her routine is not for the faint-hearted. Answer the questions carefully. Try to be funny and the DeskBot has been programmed to ignore you. Just let her call the shots and stick to the point. You'll notice that you're guest number one. This could be a clue that something odd has been going on. Or it may just be that no-one has managed to get past Marsinta yet. Don't be put off though – she's not like this all the time. If you wait long enough you're bound to encounter her in a better mood.

The DeskBot

Perhaps this is a good moment to explain how the Bots function on the Starship Titanic. As all Bots start life as "Genuine People Personalities" they come equipped with characteristics both good and bad. Special 'cellpoints' allow their owners to customise

Designer Room Numbers

Design Room Number

them according to individual tastes. Helpful dials are included on the PET to indicate if a Bot has moved away from its recommended cellpoint settings. In theory, it's a wonderful theory. Just so long as nothing goes wrong with the central intelligence which controls them. As soon as that happens Bots exhibit random behaviour which may not be pleasant to observe and which is normally suppressed. They also become decidedly unhelpful. It is possible to fix them but that is not the kind of information you are likely to find in a chapter called Hints.

Back to Marsinta. When she's ready she'll allocate you a room and your PET will ping into Designer Room Numbers mode. The coloured chevron in the Box in your PET is known as – a chevron. Logical really. It's a graphical representation of your room address. All rooms on board the Starship Titanic have one. When the check-in is over, Marsinta calls the BellBot then folds back into her desk, leaving you on your own. Not for long

Krage Koyotoaal – your BellBot

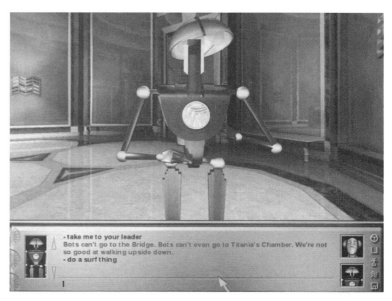

- take me to your leader
Bots can't go to the Bridge. Bots can't even go to Titania's Chamber. We're not so good at walking upside down.
- do a surf thing

> *Years ago I visited the Queen Mary on Long Beach, California. It is so beautiful and has such incredible, exquisite workmanship, very different from the slight air of Holiday Inn you get on QE2. That lodged in my mind as being a wonderfully different starting point for a starship. All starships, when it comes down to it, are really variations on the Starship Enterprise: lots of moulded plastic surfaces which you really wouldn't want to live in day by day. You watch Star Trek (and this is absolutely no disrespect to Star Trek whatsoever) and you think 'how can those people live in that environment?' All those sculptured plastic surfaces and skin tight clothes. It would drive you crazy after a while.*
> DOUGLAS ADAMS

however. An animated lamp lurches into view. Designed to blend into any elegant background this is the BellBot – Krage Koyotaal IV. Krage is supremely unqualified to be a BellBot. Really he'd much rather be on a beach drinking a cold beer. Krage is not somebody you can rely upon in normal circumstances – if his cellpoint settings drift he's even worse. To get rid of him just say goodbye – or swear repeatedly – he's strangely sensitive and won't hang around long enough to be insulted.

Now's a good time to get a fix on the geography of the Embarkation Lobby. Stand in the middle of the room on the large Starship Titanic logo and face the DeskBot. If you nav left you should see a large single door – that is the entrance to the main public areas of the ship. Nav left again and you see a box-like object with a

reflective cover: this is the Succ-U-Bus. Nav left once more and you see the main door through which you entered the ship after the Credit Sequence. On the left of that is a door which does not function. On the right of the main door is the entrance to the Service Elevator.

Let's take some time now to explore the basic PET functions. If you click the icon on the top right hand corner you'll see you're back in Chat-O-Mat mode and your conversation (if it can be called that) with Krage is still displayed. Using the arrows you can scroll back through it. The PET automatically changes into Chat-O-Mat mode and displays who you are talking to whenever a Bot is activated. If you click on the image of the DoorBot, Fentible will

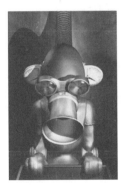

The Succ-U-Bus

PET in Baggage mode

H
I
N
T
S

return and you can chat to him. Click on the next icon down and you go into Personal Baggage mode (used to store objects you pick up); below that is Remote Thingummy mode (used for operating devices on the ship); below that is Designer Room Numbers mode (collects room addresses); and below that is Real Life mode which you use for saving games, quitting, adjusting volume and so on. Detailed PET operating instructions are on p18.

If you want to test the whole system and practise with the PET have a shot at sending an object round the ship. Go to the Succ-U-Bus and click on it. It will open with a foul phlegmy gargle. Thankfully smell has not yet been built into the Starship Titanic Experience. The Succ-U-Bus is a basic Bot, a Genuine People Personality who got the job by virtue of an astonishingly low vocabulary. Passengers are not advised to enter into

*Grand Axial First Class
Canal*

> ❝ We drew images from everywhere. One minute a wonderful hotel in Tokyo then the next minute something Ancient Egyptian. I think the Chrysler Building has always remained in my mind as being a key touchstone. It was Oscar and Isabel who put the whole ménage together – Chrysler Building, Queen Mary, Tutankhamun's tomb. They then topped it off with a bit of Venice which I thought was just a final crowning touch. ❞
>
> DOUGLAS ADAMS

philosophical debate with the Succ-U-Buses. They'll just talk nonsense to you. This is not your fault. They are simply not very bright. Their role on the ship is confined to sending and receiving things, belching and impersonating Douglas Adams.

Go to Personal Baggage mode in your PET. At the moment all you've got is your Picture of the Night Sky. Drag the Picture towards the tray of the Succ-U-Bus – it will disappear into a Baggage cylinder. Go to Designer Room Numbers in your PET (fourth one down). Click on your room chevron then drag it onto the Succ-U-Bus until you hear a good ping. Then go to Remote Thingummy (third one down) and highlight the Succ-U-Bus in the left-hand Box. Then click on SEND. The Succ-U-Bus will send your Picture of the Night Sky to your room – or at least to the Succ-U-Bus outside your room. He'll also helpfully tell you whether or not he managed it.

Now that you've got rid of your Baggage, why not do what intelligent passengers normally do when they board a liner – wander around, stick your nose in everywhere and wish you'd purchased First Class. Go through the large door to the DeskBot's right. You are now at the edge of a large public space known as The Top of The Well. (For a detailed plan of this area, look in your First Class Inflight Magazine.) If you move ahead and then right you will see the First Class Grand Axial Canal. Try and get closer and your PET will insist that "Passengers of your Class are not permitted to enter this area". See the gondola just visible beneath the flares? Don't you just wish you were travelling First Class?

Parrot Lobby

Parrot Lobby —View from The Parrot

Turn away from the Canal and you will see a flight of steps. Go straight up the steps and through the door into the Grand Ballroom.

Well, it was going to be the Ballroom. Unfortunately the ship was launched before it was ready. Talk to the Bots in here and you'll discover that they know this room better as the Parrot Lobby or Parrot Room. This is because of the workman's Parrot that has been left behind in a cage in the centre. You'll hear the Parrot as soon as soon as you approach him — in fact from now on you're going to hear him rather a lot. Before you talk to him take a look around: scaffolding, cement, dark corners, a stick. A stick? In fact it looks more like a perch. So what's the perch doing on a bag of cement in the corner? And if that's the perch, what's the Parrot standing on? Suspicious. By the way a standard rule of the Starship Titanic is — if isn't nailed down grab it and put it in your Baggage. So, in goes the perch.

In front of the Parrot cage is a TV. To check out the channels, go to Remote Thingummy mode in your PET and click on the TV icon. You'll see the TV controls appear — ON/OFF and CHANNELS. Turn the TV on and scroll through the channels. Here's another clue that the ship is not quite prepared for passengers. Channel 1 has nothing.

Channel 2

Channel 4

Channel 5

An Uplighter

Parrot in a flap

Click the up arrow: Channel 2 is showing the Weather. The pollen count is medium. The temperature is summer (not high or low, but summer). Channel 3 nothing. Channel 4 – a strange view as if from a remote camera. A room? A wall? A corridor? Channel 5 is showing a number 27. A room number? A floor number? Channel 6 and 7 nothing. It doesn't mean much now but it will. Head over to the Succ-U-Bus. On your right is an uplighter. If you move the cursor onto it the magnifying glass appears – definitely something there to come back to...

Time to talk to the Parrot. You wouldn't expect to get much sense out of a Parrot, especially a Parrot played by Terry Jones. In fact he's not talking complete nonsense. The Parrot is a great dispenser of clues: take note that he has more than a passing interest in chickens. And pistachios.

The perch looks important – it is. It's going to need more than just click and drag to get it however – first you've got to get rid of the Parrot. Time to get physical. Try dragging the Parrot into your Baggage. He won't like it but, kicking and screaming, he'll go in eventually, and the cage door will slam shut behind him. It takes more than your PET to hold down this Parrot though – pretty soon he'll escape. Leaving a feather. This will definitely come in handy later.

You'll notice that although you can't see him the Parrot is nevertheless making a din. If we leave the Parrot Lobby and then go back in again he's made his way back into the cage. How? Well it's just one of those little Starship Titanic mysteries that you are going to have to get used to.

For now it's best to forget the perch – you can come back for it later. You could summon the DoorBot or the BellBot and ask them what has happened – maybe they'd quite like to talk about Parrots, perches, pistachios, uplighters, chickens and so on... How well they respond depends upon how well you question them – and also how helpful their settings are.

The Top of The Well

Well Shaft right

There's one more thing to do before leaving the Parrot Lobby. Go to Designer Room Numbers mode in your PET. On the far left you'll see a chevron. Click on it – yes, it's your assigned SGT Room. On the right hand side of the PET you'll see another chevron – differently coded. Click on it – it now shows you what room you're in. If you drag it across to one of the free boxes in the PET you can save it. You'll now be able to send an object to the Parrot Lobby using this icon and a Succ-U-Bus. This is another useful rule: wherever you go in the Starship Titanic, check the room icon and save it – you never know when you're going to need it.

Exit the Parrot Lobby and move forward, then right. You're now facing The Well. Take a couple of paces forward – you'll see a small flight of steps. Climb it. You can now look out across The Well – you should be able to see the giant columns of the gallery which runs round it. Two of the four main Lifts should also be visible – one on each side of The Well. If you look down you can see that you are perched on top of a giant statue. Below you stretch the Staterooms – First Class on the higher levels, then Second Class, then SGT. The tracks for the four Lifts can be seen descending to The Bottom of The Well below.

Tilt up and then turn round – you'll now see another entrance which you will not have noticed when you came up the

❝ We were looking for a location for Titania. I wanted the sense that when you found it, you'd think 'oh well, it was there in front of my eyes the whole time'. I think it was Oscar who came up with the notion of it being inside a huge light-fitting: you wouldn't see it because not only is it apparently a light-fitting, but it's the wrong way up. You'd have to figure out that you're now hanging upside down. That created a problem though: if you are walking out on to the floor, then the Chamber would need to be much smaller than we wanted it to be. We then decided to make the light-fitting the tip of the iceberg: you'd come in at the top of the Chamber and not the bottom. ❞
DOUGLAS ADAMS

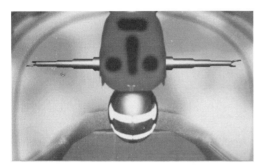

Titania's Head

steps. Move towards it. You are about to enter Titania's Chamber. Click on the door, and climb the steps. Go through the next door. You will be transported down and round on a platform till you reach the bottom. You are now in Titania's Chamber, the heart of the ship's intelligence. Move ahead – you can make a complete circuit of the room. You will pass three exits with heavy metal doors drawn back.

You should now be able to see the device which brought you down here. You will also see a figure stretched out, immobile, in the blue energy field in the centre of the room. This is Titania. Move round till you are at Titania's head. Click right. Then click down. Her head opens and rods emerge. Click on the tray which has emerged from her head: a sign appears in your PET – "It's some sort of slot". Titania is clearly important but for now there is nothing you can do – apart from make a note to ask the Bots what they know about her...

Move round so your back is to Titania's head. You are facing one of the mirrored exits. If you click on it a familiar message appears: "Passengers of your Class are not permit-

Titania's Chamber

ted to enter this area''. Go right and try the next door. This one opens, revealing a book-lined study. Move to your right and you'll see a draughtsman's desk. Click on the small screen on the side of the desk. This is the Missiv-O-Mat mail system. It's asking for a log-in. You could try a guess at whose study this was and enter a name. If you're halfway right you'll be asked for a password. And that's where you'll have to leave it for now unless you're psychic. (If you genuinely can't wait to become psychic you

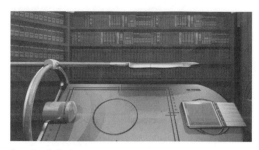

Leovinus' desk

can always go to page 144 in the Solutions chapter but it is cheating.) Click up and away from the Missiv-O-Mat and go left. You'll see a Box. Go towards it and, in spite of the warning, click. Click again. And again. The Box opens revealing a Control Panel with Fuses and a line of icons. Two of the Fuses are missing. Remember the icons – a chicken, a propeller, a tree, a coil. Each one has a switch next to it. There is also a Succ-U-Bus icon and switch.

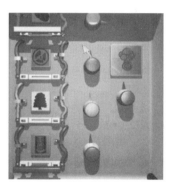

Control Panel

Best not fiddle with anything yet. Move back and close up the Fuse Box. Return to the main Chamber and you will be directed left. Keep going till you come to the next room. Enter. Unless you want a fairly low level conversation, it's best to move on from the Succ-U-Bus. Of course you could always insult him – that never fails to please. Move left – and you'll see a cheerful looking

filing cabinet with a large red button. Go towards it. Under the button is a sign: PUSH BUTTON TO DIS-ARM BOMB. Now that sounds like a sensible thing to do. Click on the button.

A Bomb

This of course is a Strategy Guide not a Munitions Help Desk. So you've armed the Bomb. Instead of looking round for someone to blame, which is of course the normal human reaction in such cases, you ought to think about how to disarm it. Clearly the idea is to move all the tumblers until you've entered a code. Question is – what's the code? No matter how clever you are you're not going to find inspiration here. Exit the room. You will find you are facing the platform on which you descended into Titania's Chamber. Move the cursor to the top right of the screen until it points upwards – click. You will now be taken up and out of the Chamber. Click again upward, sideways and then straight ahead till you emerge again at The Top of The Well.

Approaching the Pellerator

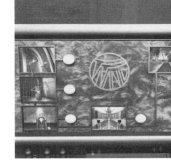

Pellerator Controls

Make your way round The Well by Lifts 1 and 2. On your left you pass a large bronze cylinder – this is the Pellerator, a kind of sideways elevator. Stand in front of it. In Remote Thingummy mode in your PET highlight the Pellerator. Then click on CALL. The door slides up and you are facing a control panel. Click on it with your cursor and you get a closer view.

There are six images of rooms. Interesting looking rooms which you'd quite like to visit. Next to each image is a button. Click on each of the buttons. Bad luck. As you are only SGT Class you are denied access to all of these but The Top of The Well – which is where you are already. So, no fun here. Exit by turning round and clicking on the opposite panel.

Keep heading round The Well until you come to the Second Class Canal. On either side of the Canal, mirroring the Embarkation Lobby and the Parrot Room, is another public room. Try to enter either of them though and you will find access is denied to passengers of your Class. Clearly being SGT Class isn't going to solve the ship's problems or give you the comfort you're used to. Getting an upgrade has to be a priority.

The Animators

For each room or character the animators would be given a detailed briefing by Douglas, Oscar and Isabel so we'd be clear about the story, atmosphere or game-play issues. Many of the environments on the ship such as The Top of The Well and the Canal are huge and it was important that we understood that scale. As the drawings were conceptual one of the challenges was continuity - especially as there's been a team of up to six artists at a time working on the ship. Inevitably, the artists brought to their environments a level of interpretation that was very individual: we had to be careful not to allow our personal vision to be out of style with the rest of the Starship Titanic. This was true even in the way in which we moved about the ship. In the end we set up rules which covered animation aspects - how long would it take to travel from point A to B for example.

All of this and the sheer beauty and style of the ship called for a sophisticated software package and rendering system. That software was naturally SoftImage and its render system Mental Ray. The SoftImage modelling and animation capabilities are arguably the best in the world and Mental Ray, its photo realistic renderer, was really the only reasonable option for the job.

Building a model in 3D in SoftImage is like designing a house: from a plan and an elevation the computer links the information together to create an exterior shell. You then have to tell the computer what the shell's made of.

I'll use Titania as an example. She exists both as a statue and as a Cyborg. As the statue at The Top of The Well, she is made out of metal so the first thing I had to do was to tell it - this is a material that is refractive. Then I tell it if it's see-through or not. If it's see-through, is it reflective like glass? If it is reflective like glass, how reflective is it? Once the material's built you give it texture. On Titania's face on the statue for example, I told it the material was a metal and then as a texture I painted on streaks of oxidation to give the feeling it was enormous. As a visual aid for that, I used the Statue of Liberty. Once that's done, you have a perfect model of an object - then you can animate it.

One of the greatest challenges was in rendering such rich environments in time. In order to resolve this we used the multi-processing capabilities of the Mental Ray renderer. Our systems administrator (and general network guru) wrote a perl script software which through a simple html interface controlled all of our rendering jobs for (at one point) up to twenty processors working twenty-four hours a day.

When working on a project of this kind you're part of a team working on an illusion that has to feel natural: programmers, artists, sound engineers and technicians must work in harmony to pull it off. There was no greater satisfaction than to see the finished product, to play the game and walk away with a big grin thinking "I had a part in that."
John Attard, 3D Animator.

Oscar did the first sketches for the ship on a flight to LA the day we joined the project. From that shape came the overall structure of the ship which was the first thing that we designed - The Well and then The Canals being the actual T of Titanic. Instead of using the real Titanic with the funnels as the key, what we used was the T of the name itself.
Isabel Molina, Designer.

The original Maître d'Bot which Oscar and Isabel had sketched was very humanistic. We decided that it wasn't such a good idea to have a robot that was so human: it didn't really fit in with the rest of the characters. Douglas gave me some sketches but they were just little stick figures which looked like Salvador Dali with squiggly hair. We knew we wanted him to look a bit like the BarBot but we couldn't really have the identical face so I came up with the idea of having it more triangular and it just went from there. I put in lots of cables to make it look as though it's in pieces. Basically I started off with one complete figure and then just dissected it.
Gillian Best, 3D Animator.

The Sculpture chamber was inspired by the work of Richard Meier the architect responsible for the State Museum, Albany, NY. Meier uses daylight to create wonderful environments for exhibiting sculptures and paintings. I originally envisaged the room as monochromatic with the play of light focusing attention on the sculptures: in the room there's a strong source of daylight and the sculptures are pin-spotted. We also used a sophisticated shader in SoftImage to give atmosphere, rather in the way that smoke is used in theatre or film. In terms of the sculptures I followed Oscar and Isabel's details closely but I was given a lot of freedom in the environment. I tried to use similar lighting in the Creators' Chamber, with a focus on the Boolean Cube. The heads were done by Cyberscanning. The pictures on the walls are paintings by Oscar.
Bernie Doyle, 3D Animator.

The lifts

G. Nobbington Froat (Nobby)

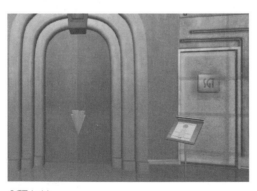

SGT Lobby

Time to go back to the Lifts and see if you can find your room.

Work your way round The Well until you get to Lift number 3 or 1 – these are the only Lifts that service the SGT floors. Your PET will tell you the Lift number when you stand in front of it. If you find yourself by Lift number 4 it's worth calling it anyway using your PET. You will get the message: "This elevator is in an advanced state of current non-functionality". Remember this – it will be useful. When you're facing your chosen Lift, go to Remote Thingummy, highlight the Lift and click CALL. The doors will open and you will be greeted by the LiftBot. Nobby, as he is called, is long-suffering. Ask him about the war. Or his Allenoids. Or even his Blibber.

When the LiftBot asks where you would like to go, you can check your room number by going to Designer Room Number and clicking on the chevrons till you get to your own. Then go to Chat-O-Mat and ask the LiftBot to take you there. Alternatively in Remote Thingummy you can click on the icon marked GO TO YOUR STATEROOM.

If you attempt to use Lift 2 in spite of the advice which you've been given, you won't be so lucky. Upon asking for a floor which houses SGT rooms (basically any floor in the thirties) the LiftBot will apologise and suggest you use Lift 1 or 3 – he only goes down as far as floor 27.

You'll notice that the ambient sound soon turns from lush First Class to tinny SGT Class as you approach your floor. When Nobby says you've arrived, swing round and exit the Lift.

You're now in one of the plush Super Galactic Traveller-Class Lobbies. Straight ahead of you is a door. Click on it. You are facing the SGT Restaurant. This should be your first clue that you are not travelling in style. Click on the little lever on the top and watch carefully: you're going to have to be quick to catch this. Yes, that was a chicken, moving faster than it ever did when it was alive. Listen carefully and you'll hear the Succ-U-Bus eating it. And according to the message on your PET it's the only one you're allowed. If you retreat from the

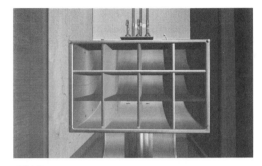

SGT Restaurant

Restaurant, it's worth taking a look at the menu outside. Clearly a chicken-fancier's delight.

Move left and head for the Succ-U-Bus. Remember you posted your Picture of the Night Sky? Now's the time to find out if you're in the right place – or if the Succ-U-Bus really did send the picture correctly. Click on it to open then go to Remote Thingummy. Click on the Succ-U-Bus icon and click on RECEIVE. After the usual complaints the Succ-U-Bus will deliver a canister. Drag this into your PET and if you are lucky the Photo of the Night Sky which you sent from the Embarkation Lobby will appear. You have now mastered the Succ-U-Bus system.

Move right and you'll see a door. Head towards it. This is the SGT Leisure Lounge. Apart from the nice picture you'll notice a Long Stick in a case. Surprisingly if you try and get this a message appears:

"For Emergency Long Stick smash glass". If you attempt to smash the glass with your puny cursor however, nothing happens. So, if you want the Long Stick you're going to have

Long Stick Dispenser

SGT Lounge

to find something to smash the glass. For a subtle mood-change, click on the picture. Sit in the chair. Relax.

That's enough relaxing. Head out of the SGT Leisure Lounge. You now get a good view of the rooms. Notice that they're not all at ground level. On the right you'll see a series of mini-elevators. To reach your room you may have to take one of these. The rooms on the bottom row are 1-6, the next level 7-12 and the top 13-18. To work out which room is which stand outside any room and go to Remote Thingummy – this will show your current location.

> " When you get down to your room, it is basically a lot of boxes which you have to sort out. I was thinking of those Japanese hotels, which are just tubes that you lie in and everything you want is within a hand's reach, but here it is mixed up with aeroplane coach class and Chinese box puzzle. Our production team always referred to this as Riff Raff Class, rather than Super Galactic Traveller Class. "
> DOUGLAS ADAMS

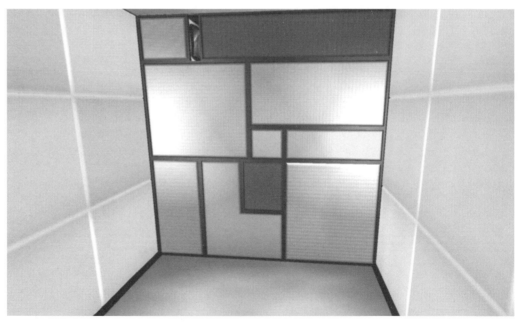

SGT Stateroom

If you have a high number take a mini-elevator – the buttons which operate them are obvious. When you finally reach your correct room, the door will open revealing it in all its splendour. Not quite as grand as you were expecting perhaps? Your job now is to open up the furniture in the right order, spurred on by the promise of an upgrade from the in-room TV. Believe it or not there is a logic to this – your main aim should be to provide a sturdy enough platform for you to approach the bed, click on it and climb up. So, look in Remote Thingummy for objects that match the shape or size of the room furniture. Highlight each object and then click on the controls. Once you've created a stable platform, move onto the bed and click on the TV which will automatically emerge. Now click on the TV in Remote Thingummy and turn on the TV using the controls on the right. Go to Channel 3 and listen to the instructions carefully – you are just one Inflight Magazine away from an upgrade. Now leave the room and go back to the Succ-U-Bus in the Lobby. Open him up then click RECEIVE in Remote Thingummy. When the canister arrives, drag it into your PET – it contains the SGT Inflight Magazine. If you look carefully you will see that by a miracle of planning your SGT Inflight Magazine looks astonishingly like the one in your First Class Inflight Magazine – only tinier.

Head back for the Lift and ask the LiftBot to take you to The Top of The Well. As soon as you're there go straight to the Embarkation Lobby

Approach the DeskBot (if possible with a level of swagger appropriate to your imminent Second Class status). Activate her by clicking. Tell her you have the Magazine. Drag it from your PET and place it on her head. (This is not normally the way to persuade a deskclerk to upgrade you but as it happens it works quite adequately on the Starship Titanic so don't nit-pick OK?)

The DeskBot will upgrade you to Second Class and you can now begin to enjoy a whole new lifestyle. By the way, you'll find that if you talk to Marsinta for long enough her mood will shift from downright murderous to oily smarm. She'll also veer wildly from curt to talkative. Keep your eye on the indicators on the left hand side of your PET and see if you can work out exactly what her settings are.

Now you're Second Class you'll want to explore all those forbidden rooms. A word of caution however. Do not for one moment believe that you are through with SGT Class. Even should you somehow achieve First Class status you will still have to return to the SGT areas to complete puzzles.

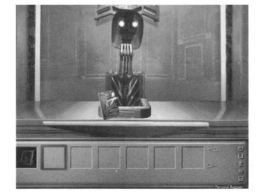

Marsinta Drewbish

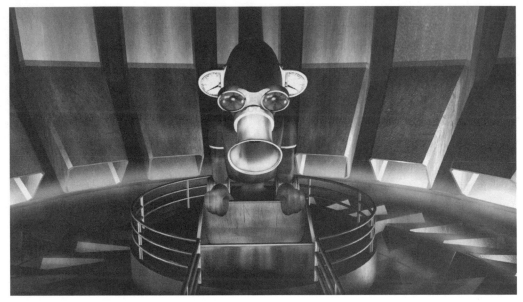

The Mother Of All Succ-U-Buses,

For now though there's somewhere else you ought to visit. The Bilge Room. This was closed when you first boarded the ship, but now the ship has taken off it's accessible. And it's worth visiting.

Take the Service Elevator. Don't bother with the bottom button — it will just take you down to the keel and there's nothing important to see or do there. The middle button takes you to the Bilge Room. This is where all the rubbish on the ship is sent. It's also the place where anything you've sent turns up if you got the address wrong.

The Bilge Room is dominated by a giant Succ-U-Bus. This is no ordinary Succ-U-Bus. This is the Mother Of All Succ-U-Buses, known simply as — Mother. If you try sending or receiving anything down here you'll find that Mother is not working. "I've got a bit of bilious build up in my throat" is

> 66 If you think of the ship as an immense garburator (I must say I would encourage people not to) then this is the bit at the bottom where all the sludge comes out. This came about after wondering where things would end up if they got lost in the ship. Well, they end up in the sludge at the bottom of the garburator. So that's where the idea for the Mother of all Succ-U-Busses came from. I could invent something here and say that I thought of it after we had somebody round to fix the garburator.
> But I didn't. 99
> DOUGLAS ADAMS

her explanation. Roughly translated this means: "There appears to be something stuck in the pipes which really shouldn't be here and which you as a gameplayer should realise is highly significant." How are you going to get this "something" out? How can you make a Succ-U-Bus perform an involuntary action? Let's just say that until you've been to the Parrot Lobby you don't stand a chance. But - you've

Meet Brobostigon

been to the Parrot Lobby. Remember the struggle with the Parrot? Have a look in your Baggage – is the Feather still there? Now just rub a couple of neurones together – think feathers and noses. Yes. Take the Feather and stick it onto the Succ-U-Bus. Now go to Remote Thingummy, highlight the Succ-U-Bus and click SEND.

The Succ-U-Bus doesn't like this. One very large sneeze ejects a body. A rather nicely dressed body at that. This is Brobostigon. It's worth calling the DoorBot or the BellBot down here and having a chat with them about Brobostigon. If you're lucky you just might find out a bit more about what's been going on.

Inspect the body: another rule on board the Starship Titanic is – if there's a body, inspect it. Click on the body until two objects appear in your PET – Titania's Olfactory Centre and a Fuse. Look carefully at the latter. Remember the Control Panel in Leovinus's study? Perhaps it's time to return.

Take the Service Elevator back to the Embarkation Lobby. While you're passing through, chat to the DeskBot. Who knows, she may be in a better mood.

It's also worth checking what new areas of the ship have become available now that you're Second Class. Head back round The Well to the rooms by the Second Class Canal which were closed to you earlier.

Second Class Grand Axial Canal

The Sculpture Chamber

Some Useful Sculptures

Try the room on the left. Enter and go to Designer Room Numbers. Click the chevron to identify – this should be the Sculpture Chamber. Save the icon just in case. Ahead of you is a giant SCSI cable. It's big but is it art?

If you move left you will see another statue. Move in closer. Remind you of anything? Go to Chat-O-Mat and take a good look at the BellBot. Play with the levers – they return to their original position but they certainly sound as though they're working. In fact, each time you pull on the lever, you'll see the indicators on the PET changing. Clearly these statues affect the Bots in some way. Work your way round and check out the next statue. Not difficult to guess who this one is – the DoorBot. Carry on all the way back

The Creators' Chamber

to the door, clicking the levers just once on each statue. You've not met all the Bots yet but you should also recognise the LiftBot and the DeskBot. If you revisit each Bot now you may notice some differences in the way they behave.

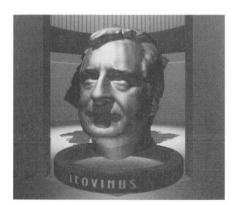

A Familiar Face

Now head across to the other room which was barred earlier. Go to Remote Thingummy and click on the identifying chevron. The Creators' Chamber. Save the address just in case.

What are we looking at here? A Boolean cube suspended in mid-air with a jumble of letters which look as though they need decoding. Move right. There's a lever. Pull it. Nothing happens. Is it broken? Maybe a Fuse has gone. Where have you seen a Fuse Box? The study off Titania's Chamber. We could go straight there or we could just look around a little more. There are three hologram statues in all – each with a view of the cube. Click on them and they revolve: Scraliontis, Brobostigon and Leovinus. The Creators. So what does the lever do? Time to go back to Titania's Chamber and try the Fuse Box.

Bringing the Bots to Life

"Originally we were intending to use Text To Speech rather than pre-recorded actors' voices. The idea was that since VelociText would be assembling responses on the fly from small modular phrases, we could automate all kinds of verbal characteristics. However, it turned out that Text To Speech at its current level of development becomes very wearing on the ear over the long haul, and indeed over the medium haul. Anything over about seven words in fact. This meant that we had to follow an alternative strategy of getting the responses pre-recorded by actors. It made an already Herculean task at least four times as big. I'm looking forward to Text To Speech becoming something you can actually listen to. Actors, I guess, are not."
Douglas Adams

VELOCITEXT

"VelociText is the language engine for the Starship Titanic. It's called 'VelociText' because it helps writers quickly bring their characters to life. One way to understand it is to think of it as part waitress and part cook, as shown in the example below.

"Imagine yourself in a diner. A waitress comes up to you with a pad of pre-printed order forms and asks what you want. You might say 'the special please', 'i'll have the special', or ' a hamburger medium-rare with mustard on the side'. She'll check the blocks on the form that correspond to the request. If necessary (mustard on the side?), she'll also write a note at the bottom describing detailed requests.

"When the cook gets an order form, he can understand many orders at a glance. The first two orders both resulted in essentially identical forms, both with a box checked for the special. The third order only requires detailed reading of the part about the mustard being on the side. When the cook reads the form, he understands the waitress's translation of what you want and responds accordingly.

"How does this relate to the Starship Titanic? Well, when you 'talk' to a character by typing on the keyboard, your message goes to the waitress part of VelociText. It does its best to put the underlying meaning of what you said into a common structure. This structure is sent to the character you addressed (the cook) for a response.

"While similar in some ways to an order sheet, the structure is organised to represent general language instead of the menu for The Restaurant at The End of The Universe. It has a set of high-level categories, similar to 'the special' box. From these, the character can tell if they've been asked a question, been insulted, or other sentence-wide notions. We developed these high-level structures to speed the character's understanding of the essence of your messages.

"The lower levels of structure might tell the character who is doing what to or from whom ('Please oil the BellBot'). For other types of sentences, it might show what object has a particular state ('It is dark in here'). This part of the analysis is based on a linguistics theory called case grammar, particularly the work of Dr Roger Schank.

"So far, all the dialogue has had to do with the activities in the particular scene, in this case, having a meal at a diner. But you'd expect your waitress to be able to talk about other parts of life as well. You can expect that from the Starship Titanic Bots too. The messages that the waitress would write on the order form are sent to computer code that represents the room in which the conversation occurs. More general questions are sent to code that represents the character itself. This is where the true personality of the character lies. Catch phrases, moods, and old war stories are woven together to provide an illusion of intelligence.

"Now, if your message still hasn't triggered a response, either based on the natural activity in the scene or on the character's personality, VelociText will go through it in great detail and give the character hints about what might be appropriate.

"VelociText handles events, too. So when you enter The Bar, the BarBot might be moved to greet you. If you insult the DeskBot, you might trigger a mood change. When an appropriate response is found, the sound clips and any events are 'served' back to you. The characters may talk, sigh, or laugh. They may shrug or even leave the room. And now the dialogue is back in your hands."
Linda Watson, July 1997
Virtus Corporation

SPOOKITALK

Velocitext was augmented with a set of conversation systems by Jason Williams and Richard Millican using their creation SpookiTalk:

"Velocitext is an excellent parser, on relatively simple sentence forms. The process of 'ticking boxes on a form' to indicate the primary information in the sentence is generally very good, but is only capable of showing as many items as it has tick-boxes - if the input is too complicated, it just can't fit all the information onto the form!

"For example, the player might say:

" 'What if I send this chicken through the Succ-U-Bus?'

"Or they could phrase the same question as:

" 'What do you think would be the result of me sending this chicken through the Succ-U-Bus?'

"VelociText handles the first question admirably, but gets understandably confused by the second. So, we applied a pre-processing system to the player inputs. This looks for and replaces common phrases that we can distil into a simpler form for parsing by Velocitext.

"We also needed the capacity to chat to the player like a real person - there is no point in constructing a façade of intelligence if the first thing the player asks sidesteps it entirely and exposes a shallow reality.

"It's impossible to totally eliminate repeats, but we've done what we can to reduce the chance of you hearing the same thing twice: the player has to (for example) insult the character frequently before we will be forced to repeat a response.

"We also put a lot of work into avoiding 'catch-alls' - the phrases that we use when we can't make head or tail of the player's input (the 'I don't understand' response). As well as matching specific questions, we added loose matches for types of questions - for example, you can ask the DoorBot 'Do you like (apples)?' and he will give a suitable answer for any object or activity you care to name. While it may not give any particularly useful information, this just helps avoid the dreaded catch-alls!

"One thing that distinguishes real people from computer-game characters is the depth of their knowledge, giving an ability to converse on a variety of topics which might not be at all related to the game universe. However, opening up the subject matter about which the player can converse changes things somewhat -

instead of having to match a medium-sized mountain of player inputs, we would somehow have to be able to match an infinite (and particularly mountainous) universe of inputs. The only feasible way out was to cheat!

"Hence, we added a database of over 12,000 'quotes' to the parsing process. If we're having trouble understanding what the player is trying to say, then we check to see if any of our quotes appear in their input, to give us clues about what they may have said.

"The quotes cover a wide range of topics. For example, there are over a thousand quotes from Douglas's books, so if the player mentions an 'alliterative residuator' we know that they're trying to be a smart-ass. Or if they mention 'Zachary', we know they're probably talking about a man, while 'Cindy' is probably a reference to a woman. If they say 'the grass is greener on the other side', perhaps they're just being philosophical. Although few people are likely to name 'balantiocheilus melanopterus' as their favourite variety of fish, the game will recognise it!

"A further feature we introduced is 'it' handling. Look at a simple conversation, and it may go something like this:

" 'What is this animal?'

" 'It is a chicken.'

" 'Can it fly?'

"Of course, the word 'it', in this context, really means 'chicken'. The character thus needs to remember any objects, actions, people, etc, which have recently cropped up in the conversation, so that it can answer questions such as:

"'Where is that?'"
"'Who is she?'"
"'What is one of those?'"
"'Why did they do that?'"

"This in itself resulted in a large database of important concepts from the 11,000 character responses, so that characters will know what it is they have just said!

"A vital element that separates a sentence from a conversation is the topic of conversation. Starship Titanic uses a 'connected discourse' system to keep track of what characters are talking about. Some of the discourse is cunningly scripted, so that we simply ignore what the player says, and continue the discourse as if replying to what they said. Other discourse looks for variations on simple yes and no answers, while a few bits are very complicated, and carefully coded to provide an 'intelligent' conversation based on the responses you make.

"The characters also remember what you have been talking about in your conversations. This allows them to chastise the player when he/she has repeated themselves, or to enquire about the results of a former conversation e.g. 'Did you find the chicken you were looking for earlier?'

"The characters are made deeper still by their cellpoints, which allow them to have various moods, and react to the way the player treats them. For example, if you are rude to the BarBot, he will become annoyed with you, and become quite unpleasant - or if you're polite to him, he will become much nicer. It's a great way of making the game more interesting, because the player has to influence the mood of the characters in order to discover vital information or complete puzzles.

"So why is it called SpookiTalk?

"Conversations between the Dialogue Team members often went like this:

"'Jason: Hey, that was a good answer to my question! I didn't make him say that - when did you do that?'

"'Richard: Me? No, I never coded anything like that.'

"'Jason: Oooh, spooky! Is it lunch-time yet?'"

Jason Williams, March '98
TDV

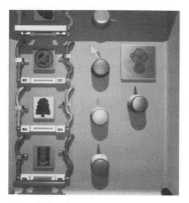

Control Panel

In the study, open the Control Panel. Is there anything which could be a hologram control? Try the bottom icon which looks like a coil – turn the knob to the right. Before you go, remember the Blue Fuse you found on Brobostigon's body? Go to Remote Thingummy and drag it onto the control panel - it fits on the second slot down. So now you know: that's the Fuse for the propeller. Wherever the propeller is. As you're leaving take another look at the desk and the Missiv-O-Mat. Try entering the names of the three creators – Leovinus, Brobostigon and Scraliontis. Each one demands the input of a password. You're on the right track.

Before you go, return to the Bomb Room and have another go at defusing the Bomb. If you click on it you'll force it to start its countdown again from 1000. So, even if you can't defuse it you can at least delay it. From now on you're going to have to make regular trips down here to disturb the countdown.

Back to the Creators' Chamber. Click on the lever – and this time watch it work. The statues collapse as the energy beam is turned off. Now go to each statue position in turn and look at the cube. The Creator's viewpoint in each case reveals a different word: THIS, THAT, OTHER. Passwords?

Back to Leovinus's study and the Missiv-O-Mat: it shouldn't take you long to allocate the correct Missive passwords. Now you can start reading the secret mail that flowed between the Creators on the day before the launch of the Starship Titanic. Your task should soon be clear – to find out where Brobostigon and Scraliontis concealed Titania's body parts and return them before the bomb goes off or the ship crashes. Of course – you do already have her Olfactory Centre. Move round until you are next to her head.

The Second Class Lobby

Click on it so the rods emerge. Go to Personal Baggage, grab the Olfactory Centre and drag it onto the head – it slots in perfectly. One down – but how many to go? Maybe it's time to find your new room. Check the address in Designer Room Numbers and head for the appropriate Lift.

The 2nd Class Lobbies are an even more pleasant version of SGT Class, with their own mini-elevators to take you to

The Second Class Stateroom

the higher rooms in each Lobby. This is where you can truly savour the Starship Titanic Experience. Enter your new room. Well, you asked for a view didn't you? Even if you didn't you've got one. Take a look at the windows. Click on one and your PET suggests "For a better view why not try the Promenade Deck?" Good idea. But not quite yet. Try the other window – this is clearly a room with a sense of humour.

> **❝** *Second Class represents moving upwards a lot in terms of desirability when you reach it but it is still somewhat generic. I have stayed in an awful lot of hotel rooms exactly like that all over the United States. One of the features you always find of rooms in American business hotels is that just as you are lying down, a parrot swoops in and steals all your pistachio nuts.* **❞**
> DOUGLAS ADAMS

There's a lot to see in here: bowls of sweets, pistachios, liquorice. Luxury. Did I say pistachios? And who else has been talking about pistachios? Yes the Parrot. And take a second look at those bowls. You're looking for body parts remember? Does this remind you of anything? Not the prettiest ear in the world but an ear nevertheless. Unfortunately these bowls won't drag into your PET. Maybe they would if they were empty? But they don't empty – you can fiddle about with them but it doesn't look as though you're allowed to eat them. Time to get the Parrot.

Head back to the Parrot Lobby. You're going to have to be on the ball here. In Remote Thingummy, grab hold of the Parrot and drag it into your PET. It will scream but just ignore it. Now move quickly to the Succ-U-Bus. Click on the Succ-U-Bus to open it. Go

Parrot meets Pistachios

to Baggage mode. Drag the Parrot towards the tray. The Succ-U-Bus will accept it and put it into a cylinder. Now go to Designer Room Numbers and highlight your 2nd Class Room. Drag the icon onto the Succ-U-Bus. It will be accepted with a ping. Now go to Remote Thingummy, highlight the Succ-U-Bus then click on SEND. And say goodbye to the Parrot for a while.

Back to the Lift and down to your room. Go straight to the Succ-U-Bus and open it. Go to Remote Thingummy, highlight the Succ-U-Bus and click on RECEIVE. You'll hear the sound of the Parrot arriving. Now go to the bowl of pistachios on the bedside table and rustle them – this will alert the Parrot to their presence. Within seconds he'll fly over and wolf the lot. Click on the bowl and it will unscrew from the table – you can now drag it into your PET where it will be indicated as Titania's Ear. All right so it doesn't look much like an ear when it's spinning round in your PET – just bear in mind it belongs to a totally artificial cyberintelligence.

Those readers with a medical degree may by now have worked out that we are look-ing for two ears, two eyes, probably a nose, maybe a mouth and perhaps some other centres to go with our Olfactory Centre.

Time to go to the Promenade Deck as the helpful porthole suggested. Return to the Lift. After you've summoned it you'll notice that one of the options on the left is BOTTOM OF THE WELL. You might as well have a look now – on the basis that you never know what might be important later and later you might not get the

The Bottom of The Well

chance. The Bottom Of The Well is very grand – the only imperfection being a small ball you should be able to see in the middle of the floor. Go over to it. It's a LiftBot Head, looking rather forlorn in such a space. In fact this is about as close to pathos as you're going to get on the Starship Titanic. Drag the little Head and put it in your PET. Check all the Lifts – if one of his heads is down here then what's in its place? It's worth noting

> ❝ We looked at the original Titanic of course. It's very attractive, but it's not exactly art deco. In fact French liners are more how you expect the Titanic to have been. We looked at 50s American electrical appliances, fridges, cookers and so on because they are all such good examples of 'Streamline'. You can see a lot of that influence at work in the actual design of the Bots. We were also very influenced by the architecture of the Modern Movement which ironically borrowed heavily from ship design. So we took architecture that drew from ships to design our own ship – you can see the influence in the exterior details of the Titanic. Oscar also looked at bone shapes, skeletons from dinosaurs and so on when he was working on the external shape. ❞
>
> ISABEL MOLINA, DESIGNER

that you can only enter Lifts 1 and 3 down here – Lifts 2 and 4 are therefore in some way connected.

Return now to The Top of The Well and try the Pellerator again. You'll find that your Second Class status offers you many more options. Go closer to the Control Panel. You now have access to all three rooms on the left – the Promenade Deck, the Music Room and the Bar. The Bar – perhaps you ought to pay a visit there before taking a walk on the Promenade Deck.

As you enter the Bar just feel that relaxing ambient sound relax you. Ahead of you is the BarBot, polishing a glass in his own distinctive way. Go over to the end of the Bar and turn to face him. There's a TV on the bar counter. Using Remote Thingummy turn it

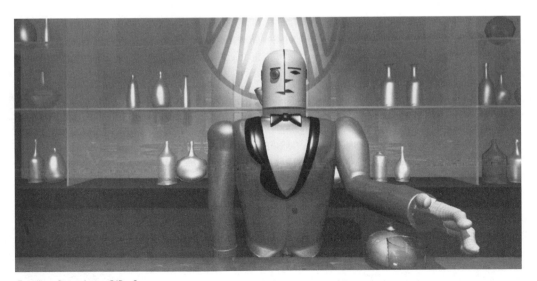

Fortillian Bantoburn O'Perfluous

Titanic Titillator

on. You'll see the ingredients for a cocktail – the Titanic Titillator. Now go to the middle of the Bar and press the bell. The BarBot will come over and hand you a glass. Do what you would do in any bar – take the glass and put it in your Baggage. Then start talking. The best place to get clues for this puzzle is right here in the bar – from the BarBot himself. He's pretty good at explaining what's happened, what's wrong, what he needs and where you can find it. When he's not lying of course. Or rambling aimlessly about his favourite sport Nib. Or insulting you. The BarBot is blessed with a complex set of cellpoint settings and you're going to have to fix that before you can be certain you're getting the truth.

As he'll explain, he's in a loop attempting to make a cocktail. Your job is to search the ship for the ingredients and bring them back to him. But why should you bother? Because on the shelf behind him is something you want – The Vision Centre - and he won't fetch it until you've freed him. So what are you looking for? Puréed Starlings, a Crushed TV, a Lemon and a slug of Signurian Vodka. Just another run-of-the-mill cocktail then.

Where have you seen any of these objects? You clearly haven't yet been in a room with starling purée on tap (although it might be worth looking again at the SGT Restaurant menu). There are plenty of TVs around the ship but how do you crush one? And you would have noticed a lemon on the loose. As usual the solution is to ask the Bots – one of them always knows the answer, just as long as their cellpoint settings are right...

In the meantime, the best you can do is to search for rooms on the Ship that you've not yet visited. Back to the Pellerator and head for the Promenade Deck. As soon as the door opens you should know you're in the right place. By all means admire the

Starlings Flying

Hammer dispenser

view, but as you reach the end of the deck and turn round — think starlings. Watch them wheeling innocently around the deck. How are you going to trap and purée them? The nets don't drag. Head down to the giant ventilation fan at the end. From the mess underneath it, something must have got caught up and squished already. Perhaps if you wait, another one might fly too close. Or perhaps if you're clever you can give them no alternative. Go to the big control panel half way down the deck. Now before you do anything, move left — you should be looking at a large cabinet with a picture of a hammer on it. This is a Hammer Dispenser. And you need a hammer — remember the Long Stick Dispenser in the SGT Leisure Lounge? Click on it. It doesn't open. Try the button on the top: you will get a message — "In case of Emergency Hammer Requirement, poke with a Long Stick". Brilliant. You need a Hammer to get the Long Stick and a Long Stick to get the Hammer. What else have you got in your Baggage? A Feather. A Perch. A LiftBot Head. A Perch? Well, it's worth a try.

Drag the Perch out and poke the button. The cabinet opens and you can now drag your Hammer into the PET. Turn back to the Fan Control. Click the ON button. The message comes up — "Unfortunately this Fan Controller has blown a Fuse". Remember the propeller icon in the Fuse Box? Time to head back to Leovinus's study — I'll assume by now you know the way.

Go to the Control Panel: if there isn't a Fuse by the Fan Control then you ought to make that trip to the Bilge Room right now and find it. If the Fuse is there — turn the blue fan knob to the right. Then close up the Box and head back to the Promenade Deck. At the fan control click the ON button. Then click the SPEED

The Promenade Deck

button until the dial reads FAST. Stand well back. If you are a bird-lover of a sensitive disposition, close your eyes and turn down the sound. If on the other hand you like seeing perfectly innocent starlings being turned into purée then turn up the sound, relax and enjoy.

The problem now is – where did the puréed starlings go? You could always ask the BellBot – he might be able to help.

So the SGT Restaurant could be a good place to start looking. Just when you thought you were through with SGT Class. If you go down to the Restaurant (perhaps we should use the term chicken machine from now on) you will find that if you click on the sauce

The SGT Restaurant

dispensers at the top a message appears: "Please place food source beneath dispenser for sauce delivery". Place the glass under the pipes and nothing happens. Now you could always try fooling the machine by sticking the Parrot in there but to be honest it won't work. What you need is a genuine food source. The logical thing to do of course would be to alter the machine so it delivered more chickens. But how do you do that? Remember the chicken icon in the Control Panel in Leovinus's Study? So far you've been putting Fuses in – perhaps you can make the chicken machine work in your favour by taking Fuses out?

Head back to your old SGT Lobby and the chicken machine. If you click on the lever now you will find that the chicken velocity has been reduced – it's easy to catch the little fellow and place him in your Baggage. Now put the Chicken under the sauce dispensers – you will have to experiment here. You may end up with quite a mess of mustard but if you persevere you'll find the right position to deliver a good slosh of what is, according to the colour, Starling Purée. Place your glass underneath the Chicken – if you're clever you can fool this highly intelligent piece of hardware into delivering the Purée.

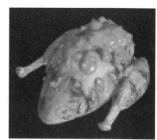

Chicken with purée

While you are still here don't forget you've now got a Hammer. Go to the SGT Leisure Lounge and approach the Long Stick Dispenser. Take out the Hammer – and smash. As soon as the glass falls away, grab that Long Stick and put it in your Baggage.

Now you've got the Starling Purée, the rest of this puzzle is easy. All you need is a crushed TV set and a lemon. You'll have seen lots of TVs round the ship. But try picking any of them up – it's impossible. You need help from a member of the crew. But who is likely to assist you in crushing a TV? Forget Fentible. Marsinta's mean enough to crush anything but if she knew it was going to help you she wouldn't lift a finger. Nobby's too attached to the Lift to help. Which leaves – Krage. A

BellBot in Destructive Mood

free spirit. A rebel. And maybe not bright enough to question what he's doing. But which TV? Why not annoy the Parrot and take his?

So – go to the Parrot Lobby, call Krage and talk it over.

Actually Krage doesn't need much persuading. He enjoys smashing TVs. Watch as he picks it up, heads for The Top of The Well – and throws it off. Easy. Now all you have to do is go to The Bottom of The Well and drag the TV into your Baggage.

Getting a lemon is more complicated. Talk to the Bots about it and, unless they're lying, the only place you're going to get a lemon is the Arboretum. Unfortunately, access to the Arboretum is restricted to First Class Passengers only. So how do you get an upgrade? Try asking the advice of a Bot. You'll get the same answer from all of them: only the DeskBot can authorise an upgrade and the DeskBot is notoriously unhelpful. If only you could change her character. Well, maybe you can. Remember the Sculpture Chamber? Time to go back there and check out the statue that looks like Marsinta...

Marsinta's Cellpoints

The First Class Lobby

Now go to the Embarkation Lobby and be brazen: ask Marsinta straight out for an upgrade. If you got the levers right then she will be disgustingly pleasant to you. She will also upgrade you to First Class.

Yes, now you are truly master of your own destiny. You are of course also still hurtling out of control through space, whilst your time is being taken up solving a series of bizarre and utterly meaningless puzzles – but that's Life.

As you glide out of the Embarkation Lobby with your shiny PET displaying your new-found status to a completely deserted ship, you will notice that access to the First Class Canal is now open. At the jetty a gondola awaits, ready to take you to the far end of the Canal.

Before that you must visit your new room. Take the Lift. As you step out into the First Class Lobby you should at last feel comfortable – this is of course the kind of treatment

Channel 4

you were expecting. Note how easy it is to find your room – no fiddly little Lifts, just grand entrances, grand style. Time to relax again and try the TV. Go to channel 4. Remember the strange view of a room and a chevron? When you look at it now do you recognise the look of a First Class room? If only you could identify the room chevron you would be able to go to the room and see what's happening.

Fortunately a small cheat exists within your PET. Yes, you

First Class Stateroom

can create your own room addresses using the CURRENT LOCATION chevron in the right-hand box. Holding down the shift key, click on the chevron until it matches the one on the TV. (Just to make things more difficult, the one on the TV is upside down.) You should find, if you've got it right, that a First Class room address appears in your PET. Save the chevron by dragging it into a spare box. Then go to the room.

PET in Remote Thingummy

In Remote Thingummy you'll see that as well as TV controls you can also operate the lights. By toggling the light switches you can tell which light is not working. To actually reach it you're going to need help. Time for the helpful BellBot again. Just call him in and ask him to reach the light for you. He'll be glad to assist and within seconds another of Titania's missing bits – her eye – will be spinning pleasantly in your PET.

After all this hard work you can now reward yourself with a romantic cruise. Go back to The Top of The Well and head for the jetty by the First Class Canal. As you approach you will see a gondola waiting. Climb in.

Your RowBot awaits

The Approach to the Arboretum

Now sit back and relax as the RowBot steers you along this architectural masterpiece. If you look up and to the right, you will see Pellerators making their journey to and from the First Class areas.

When the gondola arrives at the far end of the Canal, disembark and head straight for the woven gates. This is the Arboretum. Click on it and the gate will unfurl. Ahead of you is a lemon grove and a small control panel with SUMMER marked upon it.

The Arboretum in Summer

Click on it and in your PET you'll see: "The seasonal adjustment switch is not operational at the present time". Now there's a clue. In the meantime there's the small matter of the lemon. Take the Long Stick from your PET and take a swipe at some of the lemons. If you're lucky one will fall from a tree: drag it into your PET. While you're facing the Arboretum, move left and then straight ahead. This will take you to a small Pellerator.

In fact if you click on it, it turns out to be not a Pellerator but a broom cupboard. Inside is a fire hose and another Succ-U-Bus. Talk to the Succ-U-Bus by all means – more useful is the fire hose hanging next to it. On the principle that if it's not nailed down it's useful, drag the hose into your PET.

The Broom Cupboard

You now have the lemon, the crushed TV and a glass of pureed starlings. All you need is a slug of Signurian Vodka. The best place to start looking for this is the Bar: if Fortillian can supply it then you are ready to release him from his cocktail loop. To reach the Bar, either hop in a gondola again or take the Pellerator which does in fact come down to the Arboretum: it's on the opposite side of the Canal from the broom cupboard.

Approach the Bar and summon the BarBot. Drag the ingredients for the Titanic Titillator across onto the bar top. You can tell Fortillian that you have his ingredients but

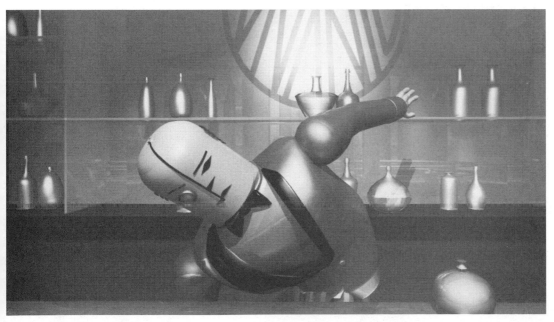

Fortillian mixes a Titanic Titillator

he'll realise anyway. All you have to do now is watch as he mixes his cocktail – and he knows how to mix a cocktail all right. Once he's finished, he'll hand you the Vision Centre from the shelf behind him – all you have to do is ask.

As you can see, the Titanic Titillator is a drink to avoid. You may want to return here later just to see if Fortillian's recovered but to be honest he's not going to be in a fit state to help.

Although you've been playing this game for hours you may have noticed that so far you've only managed to retrieve three of Titania's body parts. If it's any consolation, the remaining bits are even more difficult to find. You do however have a vast array of useful tools collected in your Personal Baggage, and you'll discover that the pace of the game increases rapidly from here on.

Step back into the Pellerator. You'll see from the control panel there are two rooms you've not yet visited. On the top right is the First Class Restaurant. Middle left is the Music Room. Let's go there.

As you enter the Music Room the first thing you notice is that there is no music. This is because the band – Boppy Headcase and his Laidback Loafers – are waiting for you to take control. As you approach the band you will see a control panel. This is divided

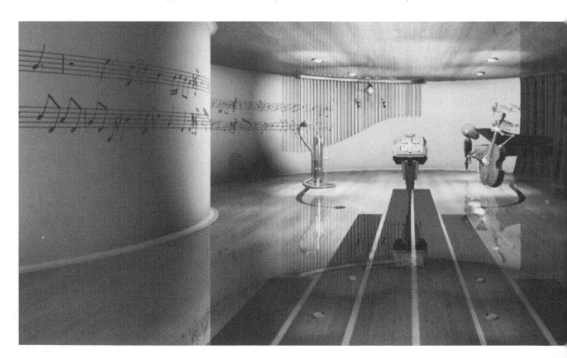

into four sections, corresponding to each of the instrumentalists. The various knobs and sliders control different facets of the music:

One changes the pitch.
One changes the tempo.
One inverts the music.
One plays it backwards.

Press the red button in the middle of the control panel. The band will begin to play. Of course, like everything else on the Ship, they're malfunctioning. Your job is to work out what they are trying to play, and reconfigure all the instruments so they get it right. If you find this difficult, don't worry. It is difficult.

Unfortunately this chapter is called HINTS — and that's all you're getting.

So how do you know when you have solved the music puzzle? Well, it just sounds — right. Like music should. If you're really having trouble then why not sit down in one of the comfortable, helpful seats in the corner.

Music Room

The Sound

THE STUDIO

Early in the production process Sound Designer John Whitehall began working with Douglas on creating the sound for Starship Titanic. He was also in charge in the studio during the long weeks of recording all the dialogue, parrot noises and Succ-U-Bus groans.

Douglas enjoyed working with John again. "He was one of the studio managers at the BBC when we did Hitchhiker for radio all those year ago. It felt very comfortable and natural going back into the sound studio and putting actors into small booths and making them say things that couldn't possibly make sense to them again. It felt like home."

Actors Laurel Lefkow, Quint Boa, Dermot Crowley and Jonathan Kydd worked intensively fleshing out the characters. Douglas was also able to bring on board some old friends: Terry Jones and Phil Pope.

"Phil is one of those people who has such a vast array of talents that most people don't realise it's the same person. He is the only person I know for whom having a number one hit record marked the real nadir of his creative life. (He won't thank me for mentioning that he wrote 'The Chicken Song' for *Spitting*

Image.) As well as being an almost infinitely better musician than 'The Chicken Song' would suggest, he's a brilliant comedy actor. He very nearly became an opera singer as well. He does a wonderfully silly performance as the Maître d'Bot, but he also instantly recognised the character of the LiftBot and got right under its skin. Phil and Michael clearly knew the same people.

"Terry Jones is an old, old friend, but we'd never actually worked together. He got so hot prancing and squawking around the studio booth as the Parrot that he had to strip off. The artistic integrity of the part demanded it, as it so often does with Terry."

THE MUSIC

"Wix is a very old friend, and I was delighted to have an opportunity actually to work with him," says Douglas. "He and I used to have the same piano teacher at school (it worked a lot better for him than me!) but I lost touch with him for years until I saw him playing on stage with Paul McCartney. He worked with Paul on a couple of tours and albums. He is a great musician and a lovely fellow to work with. He's done all the Proper Joined Up Music for the project. I've done some of the Forearm Across The Keyboard stuff (I think we call it ambient music) where we needed some late additions to the soundtrack. The one and only exception to this is the music for the Music Room puzzle, which is also by me. It's a tune that I wrote on the guitar many years ago and then later transcribed for synthesiser, and I've always wanted to do something with it. Well, if I couldn't put it on my own CD-ROM, where could I put it?"

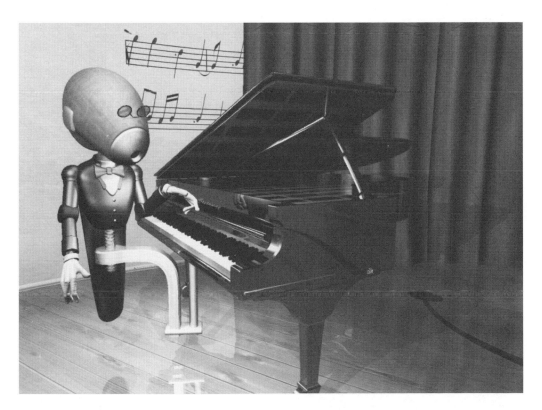

Boppy Headcase

Music Room seats.

First Class Restaurant

Head over to the other corner and you will see an old-fashioned gramophone with an ear-shaped bowl. Try grabbing it — yes it's one of Titania's ears. Now look more closely at the machine — you can record on it. If you have succeeded in solving the Music Room puzzle, you will want to record it. Believe me, you will. So, click the RECORD button on the gramophone , then go back to the control panel and set the music going. When it has finished, check that it has recorded properly using the PLAY button. Once you've done that, drag the recording cylinder into your Baggage. Your very own bootleg recording of Boppy Headcase Live on the Starship Titanic. Now all you have to do is find a use for it.

Time to visit the First Class Restaurant. Take the Pellerator — the

The Gramophone

Restaurant is marked on the top right of the control panel. When you exit the Pellerator you will find yourself in a circular Lobby. Ahead of you is a plinth. If you approach and click on it you will see from your PET that it is the Restaurant music system. It is locked. The keyhole looks conventional – make a note. Move round till you see a door. Enter and you are in the First Class Restaurant. On each side you will see tables – if you click on them you will be told by the Maître d'Bot that the tables are busy. Look around for the Maître d'Bot and he is not hard to find – straight down the carpet and in small pieces. D'Astragar, as he is known to his friends, has been the victim of a rather brutal assault but in the tradition of all great Maître d's he is carrying on regardless. Behind him is a table – slumped across it is the figure of Scraliontis. If you attempt to get too close D'Astragar will warn you off. The Maître d'Bot will talk to you but it is quite hard to avoid a fight. Whether the subject is food, menus or music the Maître d'Bot is vaiiiry touchy –

Scraliontis's table

especially if you are persistent. There is very little you can do here that does not lead to a fight. Once you are in a fight however, all is not lost. For the Maître d'Bot has a weak spot. All you have to do is listen carefully to what he says and you'll soon get to the bottom of it. Failing that you could always ask another Bot – most of them are aware of his weakness.

During the fight you'll probably pull off his arm. This can't be helped and you shouldn't feel guilty. Inspect the arm: it appears to be holding something very tightly. Something that you will probably want – for it looks suspiciously like a Body Part. Somehow you are going to have to relax that grip.

Once you have defeated the Maître d'Bot he will allow you to scrutinise Scraliontis's

Maître d'Bot's arm

table. When you get there you'll find it is worth the wait. The Maître d'Bot's other arm is on the table – clutching a key. Drag the arm into your Baggage. There is also a napkin – take it. And underneath Scraliontis's arm you'll spy a hint of bright green – bag that too. As you are leaving the Restaurant, don't forget the Music System – you've got a key now, albeit one with an arm attached. In the Lobby, drag the arm clutching the key and try the music system lock – it works. The machine opens up. But what do you do now? Well you could try Boppy's music on the Maître d'Bot and see if it calms him down a little. All you have to do is make some space in the playing slots, put in the music cylinder from your PET and click the PLAY arrow in the middle.

Go back into the First Class Restaurant and Boppy's music should be playing. It has an interesting effect upon the Maître d'Bot. It has an interesting effect upon Baggage mode in your PET too...

You will notice that you now have a new Fuse. Time to go back to Titania's Chamber and see what it does. In Leovinus's Study, go to the Control Panel and insert the new Green Fuse in the slot beneath the tree icon. Trees should be a reasonable hint as to where to go next – time for another boat trip.

At the Arboretum click on the gate to reveal the garden. Now click on the Season Changer. You will notice through the Autumnal mist an object that was hidden under the summer foliage but is now grabbable. Unfortunately if you try grabbing it nothing happens – you're going to need something to knock it down with. Check your Baggage and you'll see you've got just the thing.

If you've enjoyed this brief spell in charge of the Seasons, you may want to experiment with Winter. This won't reveal anything new in the Arboretum but it will allow you to solve another puzzle. Click on the Season Changer again and watch as Autumn blends into

Control Panel

Autumn

Winter

First Class Canal in Winter

Winter. Turn round and you will see that the Canal has frozen over: if you attempt to take a gondola you will find they're not working. However, the ice has brought one benefit. Go to the broom cupboard and turn round so you are facing the Canal. Ahead of you is a RowBot which is normally unreachable. Because the Canal has frozen you can now walk towards him across the ice. As you get closer you will see he has a very large mouth. This is a hint. If you click on the mouth however nothing happens. You're going to have to shut it up before you can grab it.

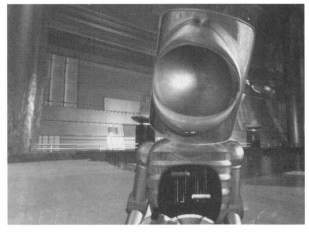

The Singing RowBot

This RowBot has a rather limited range. He can sing only two arias: since his cellpoint settings are

Spring in the Arboretum

Toscasity and Figarosity you should be able to guess where the arias come from. Unlike the other Bots his cellpoint levers are attached to his body. To reveal them, all you have to do is click on his chest plate. If you try and stop him singing an aria by pulling down on one lever however, the other lever shoots up and he sings the other aria. Somehow you need to weigh down both levers simultaneously. For which task you will need two objects of equal weight. Look into your Baggage and you will find that you have already come armed for such a job.

As soon as you have the levers under control, click on the RowBot's face again and you will find that his mouth is now detachable – it is of course Titania's Mouth. Drag it into your Baggage. Before you leave the Arboretum don't forget there's a season you haven't tried yet – Spring. Click on the Seasonal Changer. As Winter fades away and the trees come into blossom you'll notice clouds of pollen floating into the breeze. Think about this. What does pollen mean? Hay fever. Sore eyes. Sneezing. Runny noses. Noses. You haven't found one yet. You haven't seen one yet. But maybe if you move round the ship you just might hear one.

To save you wandering round thousands of rooms here's a genuine hint: the Parrot Lobby. Remember the Uplighter which activated your cursor?

Hose attached to the Succ-U-Bus

When you reach the uplighter this time you will notice that sure enough it's sneezing loudly. With every sneeze something pops up and disappears again — too quick to drag. What if you tickle it with a feather? No, it doesn't work. What you need is some method of blowing the thing out. Remember how the Mother of all Succ-U-Buses sneezed out Brobostigon? If only you could harness that awful phlegmy power here. If only there were some method of connecting the Succ-U-Bus to the uplighter. Some kind of pipe. Well there's a thing — look in your Baggage and see what you picked up by the Arboretum. Yes, a Hose. Drag the Hose onto the Succ-U-Bus. A deep Succubal instinct kicks in and the Succ-U-Bus starts to blow. Now go to the uplighter. The other end of the Hose has now appeared in your Baggage. Take this and drag it up to the Uplighter. Wait for nature to perform a little miracle...

While you're here in the Parrot Lobby it is worth reviewing your haul so far. As well as some rather dubious items that you've already used, you have a Napkin and the

Hose attached to the Uplighter (1)

Hose attached to the Uplighter

pathetic Head of a LiftBot. You are still not only looking for an eye but there is the small puzzle of the shiny blue perch to solve – a perch which is doing its best to shout BODY PART at you. By now you will understand enough of the logic of the Starship Titanic to realise that polishing Nobby's head with the Napkin is unlikely to produce the Eye out of thin air. Let's deal with the Parrot first.

What's the problem here? The Parrot won't move from the perch long enough for you to reach in and grab it. Clearly you need to find something to tempt him. There are no more pistachios. What about chicken? The Parrot likes chicken. Easy. All you do is grab a chicken from the SGT Restaurant, pop it in your Baggage, take it to the Parrot and drop it in the cage: while he's tucking in you can nab the perch and run. Just try it though. This Parrot likes his chicken hot and by the time you get it to him it's cold. He won't eat it. You're going to have to send it in the Succ-U-Bus.

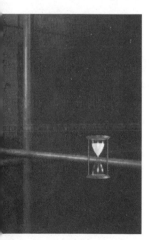

Chicken with Mustard Sauce

Unfortunately Succ-U-Buses like chicken too and if you send a naked chicken through the system it ends up being eaten. So how do you stop the Succ-U-Bus gobbling your chicken? Cover it in something nasty. Maybe mustard sauce will do. In the SGT Restaurant, place a chicken under the middle tap and wait: if it won't work try it on the bottom row. Good. Mustard appears and drenches your chicken. It also slips off.

The chicken is too greasy. So how do you get grease off a chicken? Wipe it. With what? Yes, you've got just the implement and a First Class one at that. Once you've cleaned up the greasy chicken there's nothing to stop you. Fire it off in the Succ-U-Bus and head back to the Parrot Lobby. Retrieve the chicken and tempt the Parrot by placing it just out of his reach. If it's still mustardy though, he won't fancy it. You'll have to wipe it again. When he's finally happy and you've got him munching, take the perch.

Nobby without his Head

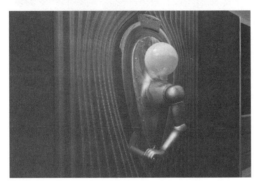

Nobby with his Head

As soon as you have it in your Baggage you'll see that it is in fact the Central Core. Do the Parrot a favour before you go – put the original perch back in the cage when you take the Core out – if he hasn't got anything to stand on you'll never track him down again.

All that's left is to sort out Nobby's head. You will by now have used Lifts 1-3 and Nobby's been all right (well relatively of course). Lift 4 is suspiciously out of action – so that's where you should focus your attention. The trick here is to work out where Lift 4 goes in relation to the other Lifts – they all have a synchronous movement. Somehow you're going to have to pull Lift 4 to the Top of The Well by taking one of the other Lifts down to various different

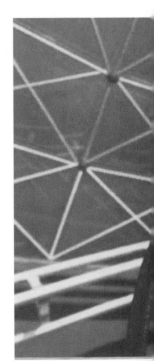

floors. Try taking each of the Lifts (not 4) down to the First Class levels and then coming back up to the Top of The Well in a different one to see whether Lift 4 is there yet. Eventually you should be able to work out which Lift connects with 4 allowing you to enter it at the Top of The Well. You'll find a LiftBot with no head but a sphere in its place. All you have to do is drag the sphere into your Baggage then drag Nobby's head into its place. Nobby will be immensely relieved to be back in one piece and you may even find this moment quaintly moving. More important is the fact that you have now found the final Body Part.

Time to fit them all back into Titania. Go down to Titania's Chamber and approach the head (as usual don't forget to delay the bomb countdown en route). As you click down by her head,

The Captain's Pellerator

Titania Awakened

the rods will emerge. One by one you can insert the Brain Pieces, the Eyes, Ears, Nose and Mouth. They have to go in the right order of course. Which is? Well that would be telling – this is the Hints section after all. You'll know if you've got it right because something interesting happens. You'll know if you've got it wrong because nothing happens.

Once you have awakened Titania and she has explained the rest of the mystery, her Chamber

Creating LifeBoat

If you wanted to write a computer game, there are three ways you could do it.

The first would be to develop an 'engine', the part of the program responsible for getting the graphics onto the screen in such a way that the gameplayer will recognize the environment as, say, a Starship, and not a collection of blobs. The gameplay is then "hard-coded" alongside the engine, meaning every action and reaction in the game is painstakingly described by specific routines in a programming language of your choice (or Java).

Coding commences on the understanding that changes to gameplay mean changes to code. Everyone agrees to never, ever even consider changing their mind about the plot, puzzles, controls, storyline, graphics, music, sound or any other part of the game, no matter how much more fun it would be, as this would require re-writing huge swathes of the above-mentioned routines.

A hard-coded game can behave exactly as described in its specification but will take approximately (give or take six months) forever to develop. The second, speedier, approach is to use an off-the-shelf authoring package. Theoretically, this provides a ready-made engine, eliminating the guru-factor by hiding away the scary system components, allowing the authors to concentrate on gameplay.

The downside is loss of flexibility - there's always something it can't do, forcing the game designer to compromise, resulting in the tell-tale 'look' of an authored game.

Unwilling to compromise, but keen to ship this millennium, we decided to write our own authoring application.

The first obstacle to tackle on a major software project is to come up with an appropriately witty codename. Tim picked 'LifeBoat' appropriate for three reasons:
1) It's the obvious means of escape from the enormity of Titanic.
2) The name lends itself to inter-capping - the IT industry habit of putting spurious capital letters in the middle of words.
3) The final letters are 'AT', allowing a retro-fitted smartass acronym ending in "Authoring Tool", which we promptly forgot.

With the project name decided, it was clear that additional programmers would be needed to work on the acronym. Tim's offer of late nights, tight deadlines and free chilled water was pretty convincing, so Rik & I joined TDV on the first day of '97, ready to write an authoring tool that would:
* Allow all authors to work simultaneously on different areas of the game and populate the ship with birds, Bots and other objects.

* Generate platform-independent C++ to wrap authors' puzzle code and character behavior.
* Plug directly into our custom-built engine, so authors could test run the game at the touch of a button.
* Represent the ship's topology as a graphical mesh of editable links.
* Map the 600 game views to the stills generated by the 3D artists.
* Link 4000 view-to-view transitions with their associated movies.

LifeBoat went live on Valentine's Day 97, and while Emma acted as project alchemist, liaising between art and science, and magicing assets into place, Adam applied his unrivalled grasp of gameplay to forge storyline into code. By Milia the ship was navigable, and the 3D starfield was tempting trendsetters to trade Ray-Bans for Red/Blue anaglyphic glasses.

Only days before, the astronomically accurate 9100-star database had been the topic of Mike's impromptu white-board explanation of quaternions to colleagues, curious to see the maths that had driven him to wear free-in-a-box-of-breakfast-cereal eyewear for a week.

While LifeBoat and its engine 'Paddle' (Pathetic Acronym Devised to Describe LifeBoat's Engine) became more sophisticated, the Bots' vocabularies boomed. Soon it would take not only three CDs to contain their verbosity, but also a veritable laboratory of language wranglers. We soon welcomed positronic brain programmers Jason & Richard, who alongside cunning linguist Renata, all appeared to use unfeasibly large plates of bread to teach the characters to talk.

The closing stages of the project loomed near, and we became increasingly reliant on sophisticated compression technology to keep within the 1.8Gigabyte data budget. MPEG-3 ensured the sixteen hours of Bot speech would fit, and switching to Indeo for the Top Of The Well navigation movies gave us extra breathing space.

3D sound gave the characters more depth, and, using the very same graphics package that the team had written before joining TDV, the good doctor Jack created the class upgrades for the PET.

As the last all-night play-testing session drew to a close, half the team retired to the office futons, while the dawn patrol began 'burning' the final set of gold CDs ready for transatlantic courier collection. Exactly 400 days after the first build of LifeBoat. The programming team wishes you as many enjoyable late nights playing Starship Titanic as we had writing it!
Sean Solle, Covent Garden, April '98.

Oh, in case you were wondering, the third way of writing a computer game? Pay someone else to do it for you.

The Captain's Pellerator arrives at the Bridge

The Bridge

“ *The Bridge is based on a notion of what happens to captains of oil tankers. There is actually nothing for our captain to do so an enormous entertainment system has been built just to keep him from going mad while the ship steers itself across the Galaxy. The ship completely looks after itself but there is a big wheel so the captain can play with it. Of course the captain isn't even there and the ship is managing fine without him so that was a little joke.* ”
DOUGLAS ADAMS

Navigator Position

seals and you no longer have access to the rest of the Ship. The mysterious third exit (which up until now has been locked) swings open and you find yourself facing the Captain's Pellerator. Into the Pellerator, and you are swept majestically towards the Bridge.

The Bridge may not be what you were expecting. There's not a great deal to do here – because the Captain doesn't do a great deal himself. You can play with the wheel a bit. Listen to the seagulls. Look at the stars. On one side there's a small entertainment centre – but the Captain's not here so you can't operate it. On the far side is the Navigator's Position. This should be of more interest to you. Because now you've repaired the Starship Titanic there's one thing left to do: go

Picture of The Night Sky

home. You don't know where earth is —
but that's the least of your problems. You
don't even know where you are. So how
are you going to get home? Easy.
Remember you looked in your Baggage a
while back to see what you hadn't used?
At the beginning of your journey you

3D Visor

picked up a Picture of the Night Sky above your house – a unique record of your home in relation to the stars of your galaxy. You're going to use this to pinpoint your home in Space – set the Starship Titanic navigation system, and return home.

Go down to the Navigator's Position and click on the helmet in Remote Thingummy. From now on you are on your own. You are going for a trip in a virtual starfield, looking for the stars that light your own particular corner of the galaxy. If you've got this far you don't really need hints. You do need your 3D glasses. In fact you need to think in threes. How else can you triangulate if you don't think in threes?

By the way. Did you remember to re-set the bomb countdown before you left Titania's Chamber? If you didn't, then you'd better not take too long figuring this out.

Don't forget the Bomb...

WARNING

The following pages contain all the information
necessary to ruin your enjoyment of Starship
Titanic. If you're reading this by chance and you
don't want to know the solutions there is still time:
go to a different chapter now. Don't leave it too
late. We'll let you reach the end of this paragraph safely but only
because we're assuming you're here by mistake.

Still reading? Well, you've been warned. You're here because you
want to be, aren't you? Because you want the shortcuts. You want
things the easy way, the way that doesn't involve hard work.
You're a slacker, aren't you? A good-for-nothing sluggard. An idling,
slouching, parasitical bum. It doesn't matter to you that tens,
hundreds – no thousands of people have spent millions of man
and woman hours painstakingly crafting this fine and complex
game. Oh no. You're happy to ride rough-shod over their feelings.
You spit on their dedication. Never mind the passion, the
commitment, the sacrifices they made to ensure the puzzles
worked. You don't give a damn.

It's just a game to you, isn't it?

SOLUTIONS

Getting Started

By all means wander around Your Lovely Home fiddling with anything that isn't nailed down. There are only two important objects in here: the computer and the picture of the night sky.

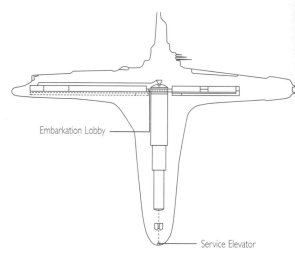

Embarkation Lobby

Service Elevator

My Lovely Home

Go to the computer. Click on its CD drawer. It will open.

Now drag the Starship Titanic CD which is on the desk into the computer. The CD drawer closes. The game starts. The Starship Titanic crashes into Your Lovely Home.

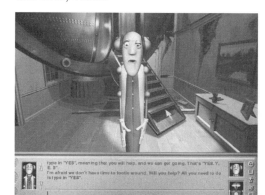

When the Doorbot appears, answer his questions and do what he asks. For PET information see p 18.

If you do not drag the Picture of the Night Sky into your PET he will do it for you.

Follow the DoorBot into the Service Elevator. Press the top button when the Doorbot asks you to. Listen very carefully to what he says.

You will emerge in the Embarkation Lobby.

Go to the plinth and press the button. Enjoy the lovely credits.

When you arrive back in the Embarkation Lobby it is now lit. Go to the desk and click on the bell.

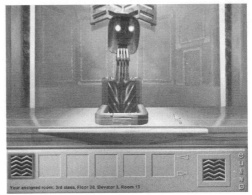

The DeskBot will appear and take you through the check-in procedure. You will be allocated a room in Super Galactic Traveller Class. When she is through she will close up. You are now officially aboard.

Getting Second Class Upgrade

Object required: In-Flight Magazine.

Whilst on the Starship Titanic, it is very important that you obey your primaeval upgrade urges.

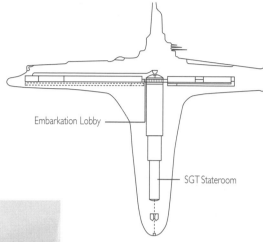

Embarkation Lobby

SGT Stateroom

Go to your Super Galactic Traveller Class Stateroom (see Hints page 62 if you cannot find your room). The furniture is now visible in your PET as icons. Scroll left or right to view. Click on the furniture in the PET and then click the button on the right to activate.

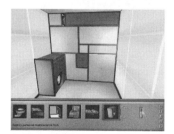

1. Open washstand.

2. Open desk.

3. Open chest of drawers.

4. Open foot of bed.

5. Open head of bed.

6. Click on bed to get close to TV.

Select the TV in Remote Thingummy mode in your PET then use the controls to turn it on and change the channel to Channel 3. Listen to the instructions.

Go to the Succ-U-Bus in the SGT Lobby outside your room. Use your PET to get the Succ-U-Bus to deliver your lucky In-Flight Magazine.

Go to the DeskBot. Tell her you have won the upgrade competition and give her the In-Flight Magazine from your PET. She will upgrade you and your new room will be visible in your PET.

Getting First Class Upgrade

Getting a First Class Upgrade is simple. All you have to do is ask the DeskBot. The trouble is, she'll only give you an upgrade when her cellpoints are at their optimum Gossipy and Sweet settings.

Embarkation Lobby   Sculpture Chamber

   This may happen at random during the game. It's simpler however to go and change them by pulling the levers on her statue in the Sculpture Chamber. Once you have a First Class Upgrade all relevant areas of the ship are open to you. In theory there is nothing to stop you completing the remaining puzzles. In theory.

Go to the Sculpture Chamber.

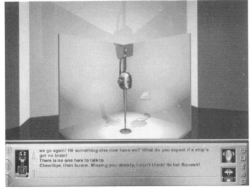

Identify which sculpture represents the DeskBot.

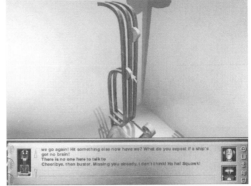

Activate both levers once: this triggers her optimum cellpoint settings.

Go directly to the Embarkation Lobby. Don't dawdle or her cellpoints may change again.

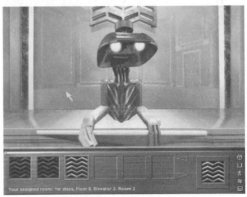

Ask the DeskBot to upgrade you to First Class. She will. Your new First Class Room will appear as a chevron in your PET.

Getting the Central Core

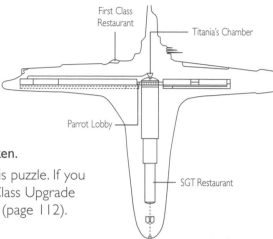

First Class Restaurant

Titania's Chamber

Parrot Lobby

SGT Restaurant

Other objects required: Napkin; Hot Chicken.

You must have First Class access to solve this puzzle. If you are not yet upgraded, see Getting Second Class Upgrade (page 110) and Getting First Class Upgrade (page 112).

Go to the Parrot Lobby. In Remote Thingummy mode, drag the Parrot Lobby room chevron into a box in your PET to save.

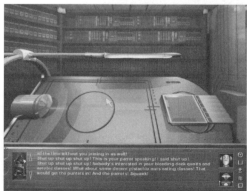

Go to Leovinus's room in Titania's Chamber. (If you're not sure how to get there see page 57 Hints).

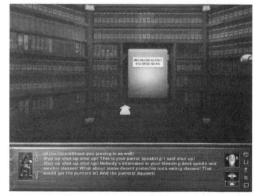

Locate the Control Panel. Open it.

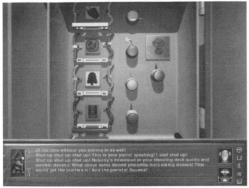

Switch the yellow Chicken lever to slow, as shown.
Remove the Yellow Fuse.

Go to the First Class Restaurant.

Poke the Maître d'Bot on the buttocks until he
says "Enfin... Enough etc."

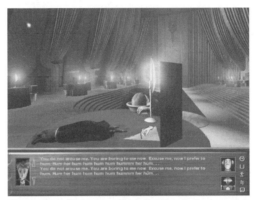

Go to the table upon which Scraliontis is slumped.

Drag the Napkin from the table into
your Baggage.

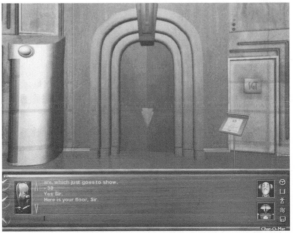

Go to the SGT Restaurant.

Pull the Chicken lever.

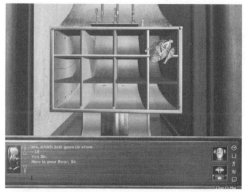

Catch the Chicken.

Grab the Napkin with your cursor and "wipe" the grease from the Chicken.

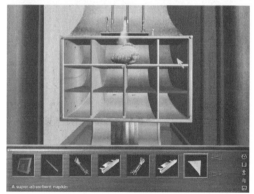

Put the Chicken in a box on the bottom row, 3rd column from the left. Mustard sauce will now squirt out and stick to the Chicken. Put the Chicken in your baggage.

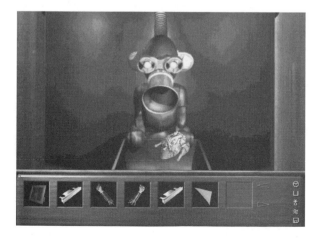

Go to the Succ-U-Bus in the SGT Lobby. With your PET in Remote Thingummy mode, send the mustardy Chicken to the Parrot Room.

Return to the Parrot Lobby.

If you do not already have it, take the Perch from the cement bags.

Remove the Chicken from the Succ-U-Bus and wipe the Mustard off with the Napkin.

Drag the Chicken to the left-hand side of the Parrot Cage. The Parrot will start to eat the Chicken.

Grab the Central Core (masquerading as a perch) and place it in your Baggage. Replace it with the real Perch to stop the Parrot flying away.

S O L U T I O N S

Getting Ear I

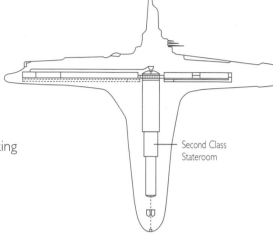

Second Class
Stateroom

If you have not yet been upgraded see Getting
Second Class Upgrade (page 110).

Go to the Parrot Lobby.

Grab the Parrot and drag him into your PET.

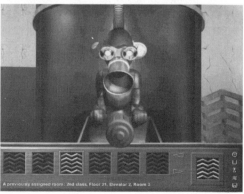

Go directly to the Succ-U-Bus and drag the Parrot
into the tray. Using the icon address in your PET
send the Parrot to your Second Class Stateroom.

Go to your Second Class Stateroom.

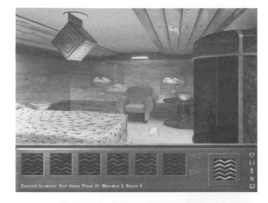

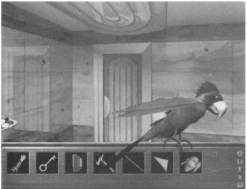

Let the Parrot out of the Succ-U-Bus by pressing
RECEIVE.

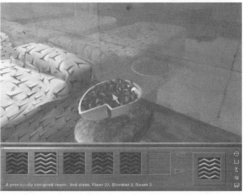

Go and rustle the bowl of pistachios with your
cursor.

This will cause the Parrot to fly to the bowl and
eat all the nuts.

The empty bowl is Ear 1. Unscrew it and drag it
into your Baggage.

Getting Ear 2

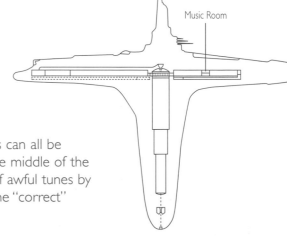

Music Room

Boppy Headcase and His Laidback Loafers can all be controlled from the conductor stand in the middle of the room. You can create an infinite number of awful tunes by manipulating the switches. There is only one "correct" version.

Go to the Music Room.

This is what all the knobs, sliders and switches actually do:

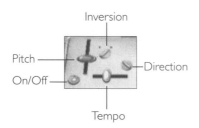

Inversion

Pitch

On/Off

Direction

Tempo

Saved Chevron: The Music Room

If you want to do it the easy way, here's how:

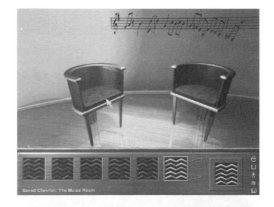

Go to the red chairs and note the pattern on the seat.

Go to the conductor stand and press the red button to turn on the music. Move the levers until the pattern matches the pattern on the seat. The music is now exactly as Boppy intended.

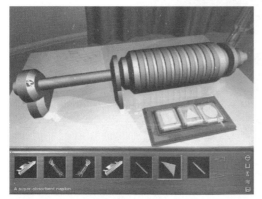

Go to the gramophone in the far corner of the Music Room and press RECORD (circle). You have recorded the music.

Pick up Ear 2 from the Gramophone.

Getting Eye 1

You must have First Class access to solve this puzzle. If you are not yet upgraded, see Getting Second Class Upgrade (page110) and Getting First Class Upgrade (page112).

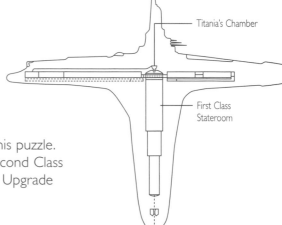

Titania's Chamber

First Class Stateroom

Go to any First Class Stateroom.

Turn on the TV and go to Channel 4. Note the chevron pattern on the screen (beware, the chevron is upside down).

Select Designer Room Numbers mode in your PET. Hold down the SHIFT key and click on the lines of the "Current Location" until the pattern matches that on the screen. Save this code.

Your PET will now tell you the room code for the chevron you have created.

Go to the room indicated.

Summon the BellBot. Ask him to get the top left light. Eye 1 will appear in your Baggage.

Go to Remote Thingummy mode in your PET. Toggle the light switches until you can see the light which is not working. This is Eye 1.

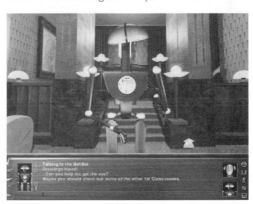

Getting Eye 2

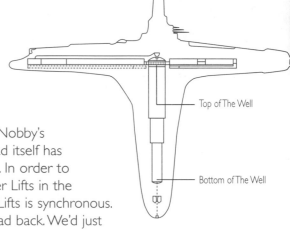

Top of The Well

Bottom of The Well

Eye 2 has been unpleasantly inserted into Nobby's head-space in the faulty Lift 4. Nobby's head itself has been discarded at The Bottom of The Well. In order to access Lift 4 you need to position the other Lifts in the correct sequence — the movement of the Lifts is synchronous. You don't actually need to put Nobby's head back. We'd just rather you did.

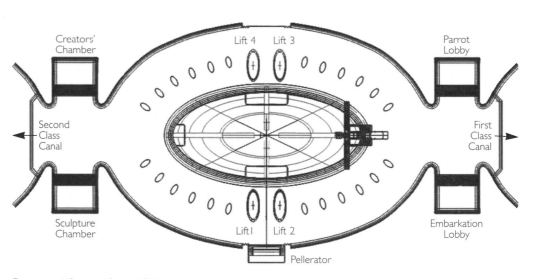

Creators' Chamber

Lift 4   Lift 3

Parrot Lobby

Second Class Canal

First Class Canal

Sculpture Chamber

Lift 1   Lift 2

Embarkation Lobby

Pellerator

Enter any Lift apart from Lift 4.

Go to The Bottom of The Well.

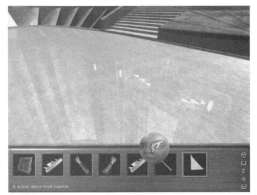

Drag LiftBot's spare head into Baggage.

Return to The Top of The Well and enter Lift 2. Descend to any First Class Floor. Exit and enter Lift 1. Go back to The Top of The Well.

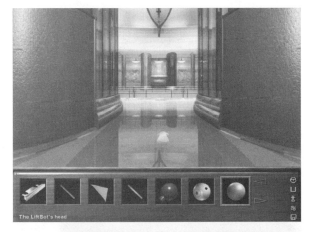

Now enter Lift 4 (the faulty one). Remove Eye 2 which is masquerading as the LiftBot's head and place it in your Baggage. Drag the LiftBot's spare head from your Baggage and put it in place of Eye 2.

Lift 4 will now function.

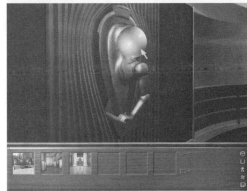

Getting the Mouth

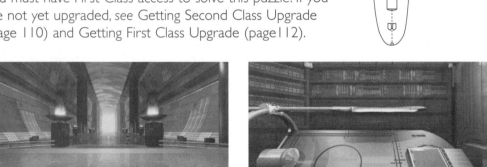

Grand Axial Canal
First Class

Titania's Chamber

Arboretum

**Other objects required: Green Fuse; Maître d'Bot's
arms with empty hands.**

You must have First Class access to solve this puzzle. If you
are not yet upgraded, see Getting Second Class Upgrade
(page 110) and Getting First Class Upgrade (page 112).

Go to the Grand Axial Canal First Class.

If the Canal is not frozen, go to Leovinus's room in
Titania's Chamber.

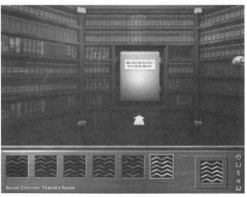

Open up the Control Panel in the alcove.

If you have the Green Fuse in your Baggage, insert
it under the Arboretum (tree) icon and turn the
switch to the right as shown. If you do not have
the Fuse see Getting the Fuses (page 142).

Go to the Arboretum.

Set the Seasonal Adjustment lever to Winter.

Go back to the Grand Canal First Class. Locate the broom closet, then approach the singing RowBot directly. (This is the only route which will allow you to get close to the RowBot.)

Open the RowBot's chest by clicking on the chest plate. Take both of the Maître d'Bot's arms from your Baggage and hang one on each of the RowBot's levers. His Mouth will become detached. If you do not have the Maître d'Bot's arms see Getting the Auditory Centre (page 152).

Drag the Mouth into your Baggage.

Getting the Nose

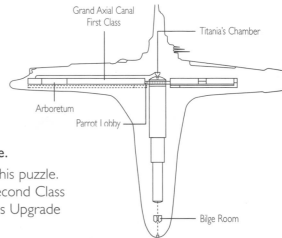

Other objects required: Green Fuse; Hose.

You must have First Class access to solve this puzzle. If you are not yet upgraded, see Getting Second Class Upgrade (page 110) and Getting First Class Upgrade (page 112).

Go to the Arboretum.

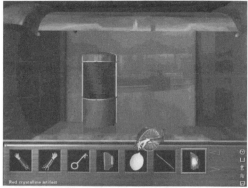

Go to the Broom Cupboard and drag the Hose into your Baggage.

At the Arboretum, locate the Seasonal Adjustment switches. Change the setting to Spring.

If the Season does not change:

Go to Leovinus's room in Titania's Chamber.

Open up the Control Panel in the alcove.

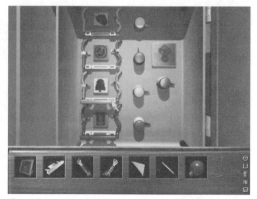

If you have the Green Fuse in your Baggage, insert it under the Arboretum (tree) icon and turn the switch to the right as shown. If you do not have the Fuse see Getting the Fuses (page 142).

Return to the Arboretum and change the setting.
A cloud of pollen will be released.

Go to the Parrot Lobby.

The Nose can now be heard sneezing, concealed
in an Uplighter.

Take the I lose from your Baggage, drag
it to the Succ-U-Bus and attach.

Attach the other end of the Hose to
the sneezing Uplighter.

The Nose will be blown in the air and
will land on the rim of the Uplighter.
Drag it into your Baggage.

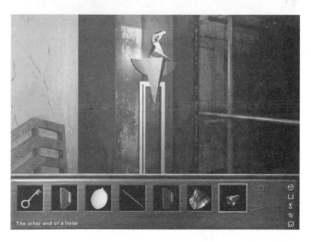

Getting the Olfactory Centre

The Olfactory Centre is concealed in the pocket of Brobostigon, the Project Manager. Brobostigon is concealed in the Mother of all Succ-U-Buses in the Bilge Room.

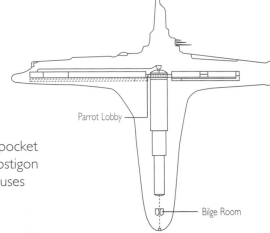

Parrot Lobby

Bilge Room

Go to the Parrot Lobby.

Drag the Parrot into your PET. After a short delay he will escape leaving behind a feather in your Baggage.

Go to the Bilge Room. Turn on the Succ-U-Bus.

Drag the feather from your Baggage onto the Succ-U-Bus tray, press SEND and stand well back.

The Project Manager, Brobostigon, will be ejected from the Succ-U-Bus.

Go to the body of Brobostigon and click on it drag the Olfactory Centre from his pocket and into your Baggage.

Getting the Speech Centre

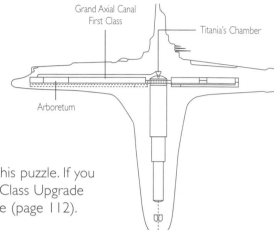

Grand Axial Canal
First Class

Titania's Chamber

Arboretum

Objects required: Long Stick

You must have First Class access to solve this puzzle. If you are not yet upgraded, see Getting Second Class Upgrade (page 110) and Getting First Class Upgrade (page 112).

Go to the Arboretum.

Locate the Seasonal Adjustment switches. Change the setting to Autumn.

If the Season does not change:

Go to Leovinus's room in Titania's Chamber.

Open up the Control Panel in the alcove.

If you have the Green Fuse in your Baggage, insert it under the Arboretum (tree) icon and turn the switch to the right as shown. If you do not have the Fuse see Getting the Fuses (page 142).

Go back to the Arboretum and change the setting. The Speech Centre will now be visible in a tree. Using your Long Stick, knock the Speech Centre out of the tree and drag it into your Baggage. If you do not have a Long Stick, see Getting the Long Stick (page 146).

Getting the Vision Centre

Grand Axial Canal
First Class
Titania's Chamber
Promenade Deck
Arboretum
Parrot Lobby
Bar
Top of The Well
SGT Restaurant
Bottom of The Well

Objects required: Long Stick; Blue Fuse; Hot Chicken.

This is a three-part puzzle requiring access to First and Second Class Areas. If you are not yet upgraded, see Getting Second Class Upgrade (page 110) and Getting First Class Upgrade (page 112).

The Vision Centre is concealed behind the Bar. The BarBot is unable to hand it to you however until you have helped him. He is trapped in a Cocktail-Making Loop attempting to put together a Titanic Titillator, the vital ingredients of which are: a Lemon, a Puréed Flock of Starlings, and a Crushed Television. Your task is to find these. The BarBot himself will add the final ingredient – Signurian Vodka.

THE LEMON

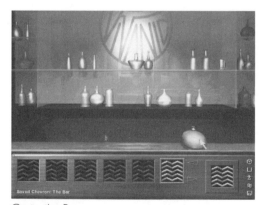

Go to the Bar.

Ring the bell on the Bar by clicking on it. The BarBot will appear and give you a glass. Drag it into your Baggage.

Go to the Arboretum. Ensure the Season is set to Summer. If it is not, only you can have changed it so you will know what to do.

Using the Long Stick from your Baggage, knock the Lemon off the tree. If you do not have a Long Stick see Getting Long Stick page146. Drag the Lemon into your Baggage.

THE PURÉED FLOCK OF STARLINGS

Go to the Promenade Deck.

Go to the fan switch and press the ON button once.

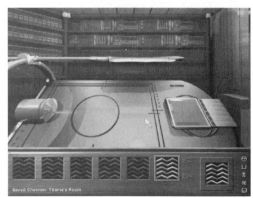

If this does not function, go to Leovinus's room in Titania's Chamber.

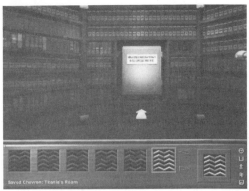

Open up the Control Panel in the alcove.

If you have the Blue Fuse in your Baggage, insert it under the Promenade Deck (fan) icon and turn the blue knob to the right. If you do not have the Blue Fuse see Getting the Fuses (page 142).

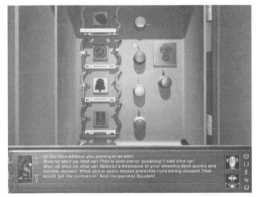

Check that the yellow knob is also turned to the right as shown. Remove the Yellow Fuse under the Chicken icon and place it in your Baggage.

Go back to the Promenade Deck. Press the ON button once. Press the SPEED button twice.

Watch the starlings being puréed.

Go to the Super Galactic Traveller Class Restaurant.

Pull the Chicken Machine lever. Catch the Chicken. (To catch the Chicken see Getting the Central Core page 114).

Place the Chicken in the position shown under the bird sauce dispenser. Purple Puréed Starling Sauce will spray out.

Quickly drag the Glass from your Baggage and place it under the Chicken. Puréed Flock of Starlings will now slide off the slippy Chicken and into the Glass. Drag it into your Baggage.

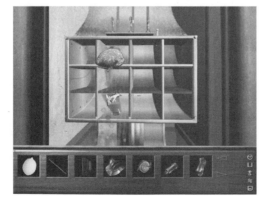

CRUSHED TELEVISION SET

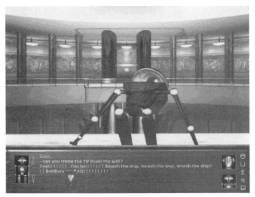

Go to the Parrot Room. Summon the BellBot. Tell the BellBot to pick up the television and take it to The Top of The Well. At The Top of Well, tell the BellBot to throw the television off.

Enter any Lift and go to The Bottom of The Well. Drag the broken pieces of the television into your Baggage.

ON COMPLETION OF ALL THE ABOVE

Go to the Bar. Drag the ingredients from your Baggage to the BarBot. The BarBot will ask "What's this?" You must reply "Puréed Starling" or something similar. Ask the BarBot for the vodka.

Watch the BarBot mix the Cocktail.

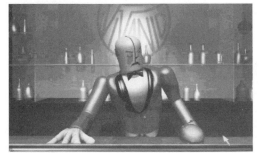

Ask the BarBot for the Vision Centre and he will get it for you.

Drag it into your Baggage.

Getting the Fuses

The Fuses belong in the control panel in Titania's Chamber. They were removed by Scraliontis and Brobostigon.

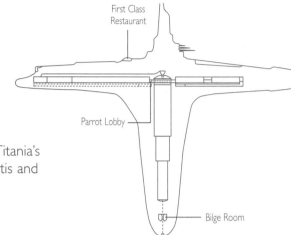

First Class
Restaurant

Parrot Lobby

Bilge Room

FUSE 1 (GREEN)

Go to the First Class Restaurant. If you are not yet upgraded, see Getting Second Class Upgrade (page 110) and Getting First Class Upgrade (page 112).

Start a fight with the Maître d'Bot. Defeat the Maître d'Bot by wounding him in the bottom. (He will say "Enfin, enough etc".)

Go to the table where the body of Scraliontis is slumped. Drag the Green Fuse from under his hand into your Baggage.

FUSE 2 (BLUE)

Go to the Parrot Lobby.

Drag the Parrot into your PET. When he escapes, a feather remains in the Baggage.

Go to the Bilge Room.

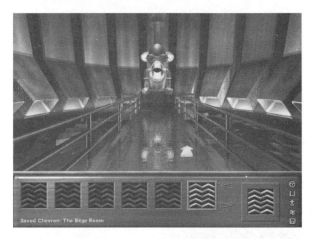

Turn on the Succ-U-Bus. Drag the feather from your Baggage onto the Succ-U-Bus tray, press DELIVER and stand well back.

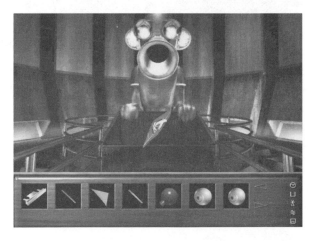

The Project Manager, Brobostigon, will be ejected from the Succ-U-Bus. Click on his body twice where your cursor turns into a magnifying glass.

The Blue Fuse will now appear in your Baggage.

Getting the Long Stick

You must have First Class access to solve this puzzle. If you are not yet upgraded, see Getting Second Class Upgrade (page 110) and Getting First Class Upgrade (page 112).

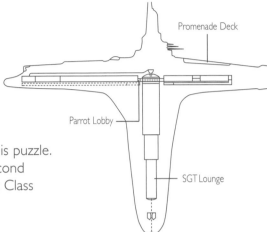

Promenade Deck

Parrot Lobby

SGT Lounge

Go to the Parrot Lobby.

Locate the Perch and drag it into your Baggage.

Go to the Promenade Deck.

Locate the Hammer Dispenser. Use the spare Perch to hit the blue button on the Hammer Dispenser.

Take the Hammer and drag it into your Baggage.

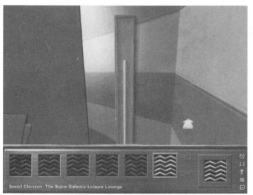

Go to any Super Galactic Traveller Class Lounge. Locate the Long Stick Dispenser.

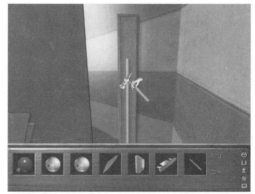

Take the Hammer from your Baggage and use it to smash the glass on the Dispenser.

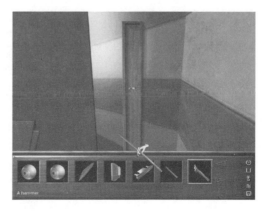

Drag the Long Stick into your Baggage.

Getting the E-mail Passwords

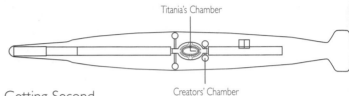

Titania's Chamber

Creators' Chamber

If you are not yet upgraded, see Getting Second Class Upgrade (page110).

Go to Leovinus's room in Titania's Chamber.

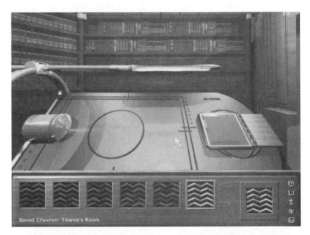

Open up the Control Panel.

Beside the red icon is a red switch. Turn it thus:

DO NOT TOUCH THE RED FUSE!

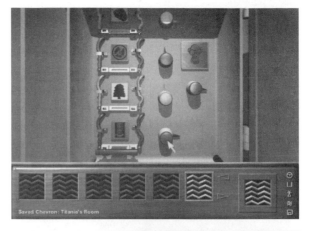

Go to the Creators' Chamber.

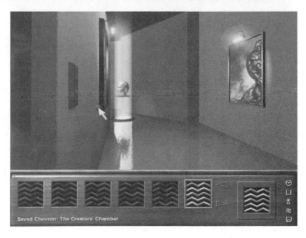

Pull the lever by the door. This switches off the beam.

Stand on each of the remains of the busts and read the passwords which are:

THIS

THAT

OTHER

Go back to Titania's
Chamber and go into
Leovinus's study.

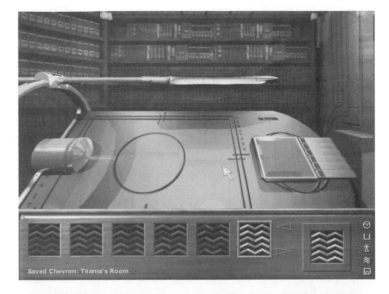

Zoom in on the desk. Log
in as one of the Creators:

Scraliontis – THIS

Brobostigon – THAT

Leovinus – OTHER

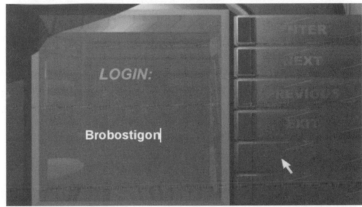

You will now be able to
read their mail.

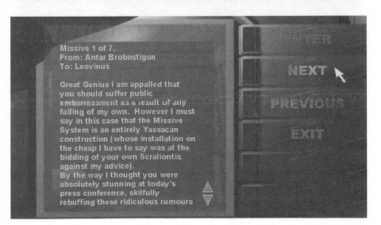

Getting the Auditory Centre

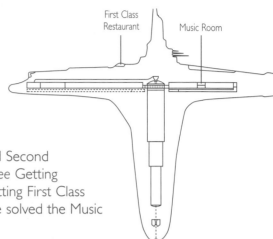

First Class
Restaurant

Music Room

To complete this puzzle you need First and Second
Class access. If you are not yet upgraded, see Getting
Second Class Upgrade (page 110) and Getting First Class
Upgrade (page 112). You also need to have solved the Music
puzzle, see Getting Ear 2 (page 120).

Go to the Music Room.

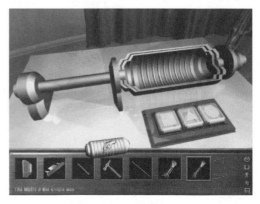

Drag the Music Cylinder with the correct
recording into your Baggage.

Go to the First Class Restaurant.

Engage the Maître d'Bot in a fight. One of his arms will appear clutching the Auditory Centre. Drag it into your Baggage. Defeat the Maître d'Bot by wounding him in the bottom. (You will hear him say "Enfin, enough etc.")

Go to the table where the body of Scraliontis is slumped. The Maître d'Bot's other arm is on the table, a key in its hand. Drag the arm (with key) into your Baggage.

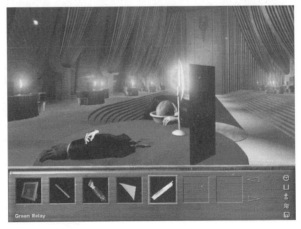

Go to the Lobby outside the First Class Restaurant and locate the Music System.

Unlock the cover of the Music System using the arm (with the key) from your Baggage.

Drag out the old Music Cylinder and put it in the right hand slot.

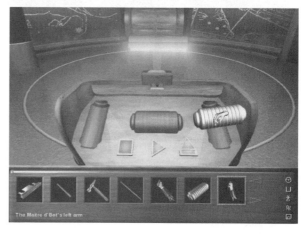

Drag the Music Cylinder from your Baggage into the centre slot.

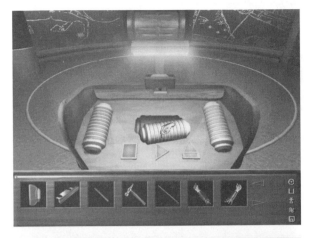

Press PLAY. You will hear your recording of Boppy and His Laidback Loafers.

Go back to the First Class Restaurant The new music will make the Maître d'Bot relax. The Auditory Centre will be released from the hand and will appear in your Baggage.

Defusing the Bomb

Titania's Chamber

If you have pressed the DISARM BOMB button in Titania's Chamber then you will know that this button actually arms the bomb. You will therefore need to disarm it. This is simple.

Go to the Bomb Area in Titania's Chamber.

Using your cursor, click the letters on the bomb until it reads:...

NOBODY LIKES A SMARTASS

Waking Titania

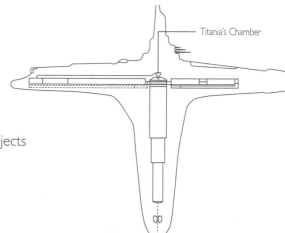

Titania's Chamber

When you have solved all the puzzles on the Starship Titanic you will have all the objects necessary to restore Titania to life.

Go to Titania's Chamber

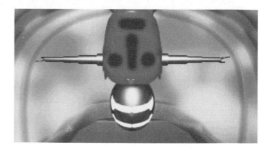

Go to Titania's head and click on it.

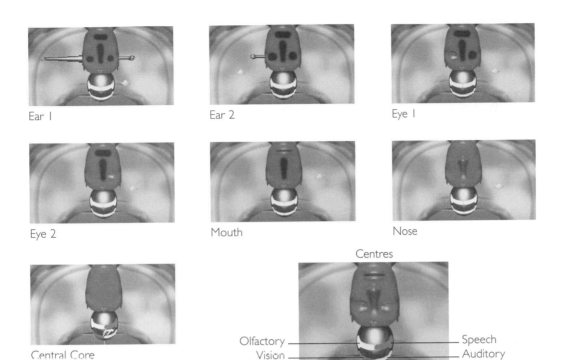

Ear 1

Ear 2

Eye 1

Eye 2

Mouth

Nose

Central Core

Centres

Olfactory —————— Speech
Vision —————— Auditory

Titania will now wake and speak to you.

Oh yes. And there is one more puzzle to come…

Getting Home

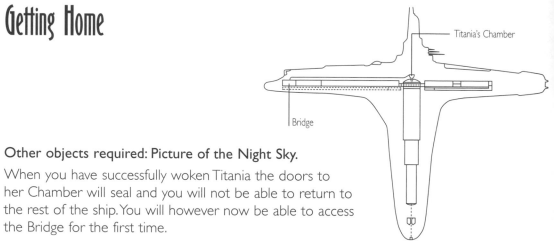

Titania's Chamber

Bridge

Other objects required: Picture of the Night Sky.

When you have successfully woken Titania the doors to her Chamber will seal and you will not be able to return to the rest of the ship. You will however now be able to access the Bridge for the first time.

In Titania's Chamber, go through the glass doors which until now have been closed.

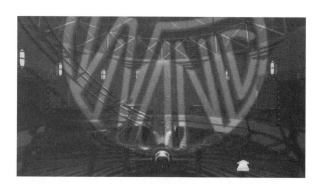

Climb aboard the Captain's Pellerator.

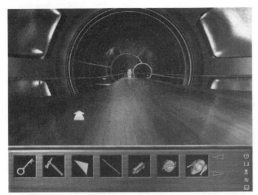

This will automatically take you to the Bridge.

Go to the top of the Bridge and then turn right.

Go down the steps and face the Navigator's helmet and table.

Take your Picture of the Night Sky from your Baggage and place it in the slot in the table. It will be scanned. If you have lost your Picture of the Night Sky, see Lost and Found (page 167).

Go to Remote Thingummy mode in your PET. Select the Navigator helmet. The helmet will come forward and drop down over your head.

You are now looking at a 3D virtual star system.

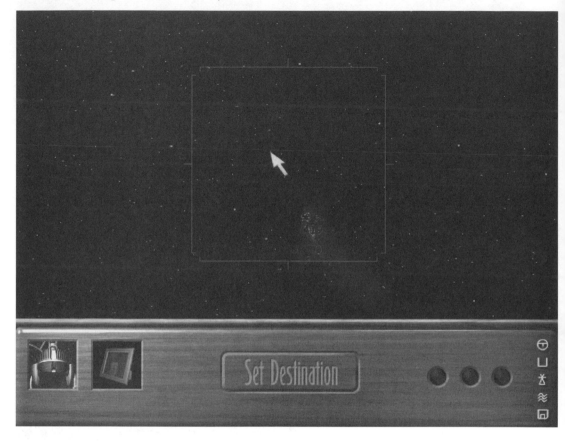

Put on the 3D glasses to view it correctly in 3D.

Using this star system in conjunction with the Picture of the Night Sky taken from above your house, you will be able to navigate back to Earth. The principle is simple. If you can find a view of the stars in the virtual starfield which exactly corresponds to the view of the stars in your Picture then you will have found the location of your Lovely Home. All you have to do is lock onto that view, go to the Steering Wheel, click GO and you will be taken home.

First get used to virtual navigation. As you move the cursor outside the central box, the starfield will rotate. Click on any star in the Virtual View and you will appear to fly towards it. The Starship of course will remain stationary until you complete the navigation and actually instruct her to move.

You can toggle between the
3D Virtual View and the
Photo View by pressing the
<return> key.

Select a star in the Photo View and click on it. The same star will be
highlighted in the Virtual View. Go to Virtual View and look for it. As you
approach it, a tractor beam will appear and join the virtual star to the one in
your Picture. One of the starfield LED indicators will also flash. Click on the
LED to lock the two stars together.

S O L U T I O N S

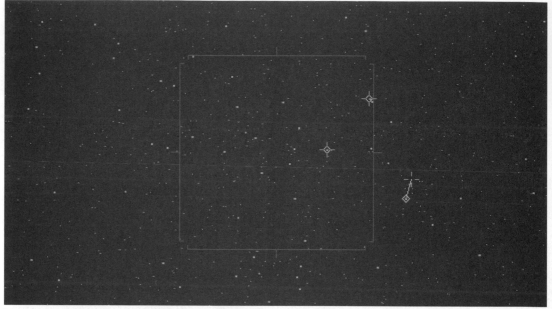

Now repeat the process with two more stars until you have triangulated your position.

As you complete the alignment of the third star
you will find the Picture and the starfield align
perfectly.

Press SET DESTINATION. The engines will start and tick over.

Now click on the helmet icon in Remote Thingummy mode. The helmet will withdraw.

Go up the steps to the Steering Wheel. Click the GO button. The engines will rev up.

Sit back and enjoy the End of the Game...

Icons Key

Centres: Olfactory
(yellow), Speech
(red), Vision (blue),
Auditory (green).

Central Core.

Ear.

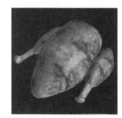

Eye.

Nose.

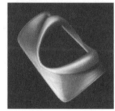

Mouth.

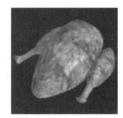

Chicken greasy.

Chicken no grease.

Chicken with sauce:
tomato, mustard,
starling.

Hose.

Hose end.

Key.

Lemon.

Feather.

Fuse: blue, green, red,
yellow.

Glass with tomato
sauce; mustard sauce;
starling purée.

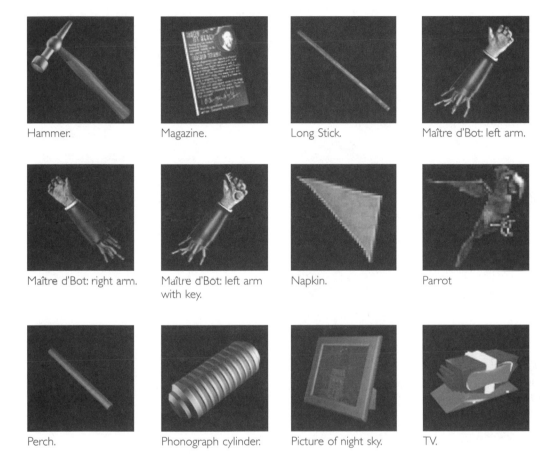

Hammer.

Magazine.

Long Stick.

Maître d'Bot: left arm.

Maître d'Bot: right arm.

Maître d'Bot: left arm with key.

Napkin.

Parrot

Perch.

Phonograph cylinder.

Picture of night sky.

TV.

LOST AND FOUND

If you have sent something through the Succ-U-Bus system but lost it, there is a fail-safe. Go to the Control Panel in Leovinus's Study. Turn the Succ-U-Bus switch to the right. Now go to the Bomb Room. Activate the Succ-U-Bus. Click RECEIVE. Your lost object will be delivered.

Cellpoints

To change a Bot's cellpoint settings, locate the appropriate statue in the Sculpture Chamber and pull once on each lever. For all Bots the cellpoint setting is High when the needle in the PET points up and Low when the needle points down. In all cases:

Setting 1 is the top dial in the PET
Setting 2 is the middle dial in the PET
Setting 3 is the bottom dial in the PET

BarBot

Ability to Come to the Point. (Bottom

Charm. (Top dial).

Honesty. (Middle dial).

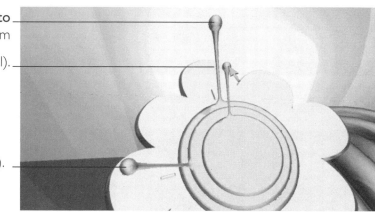

BellBot

Helpfulness. (Top dial).

Just Passing Through. (Middle dial).

DeskBot

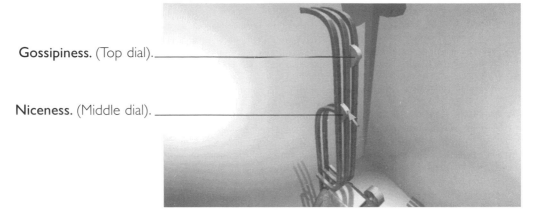

Gossipiness. (Top dial).

Niceness. (Middle dial).

DoorBot

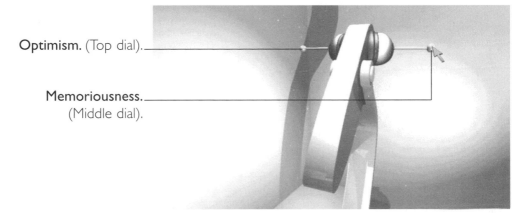

Optimism. (Top dial).

Memoriousness.
(Middle dial).

LiftBot

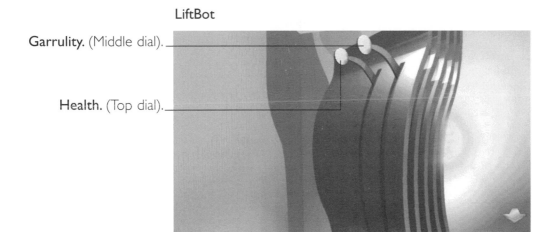

Garrulity. (Middle dial).

Health. (Top dial).

Index

Numbers in **bold** refer to illustrations

HINTS

Plans of the Ship

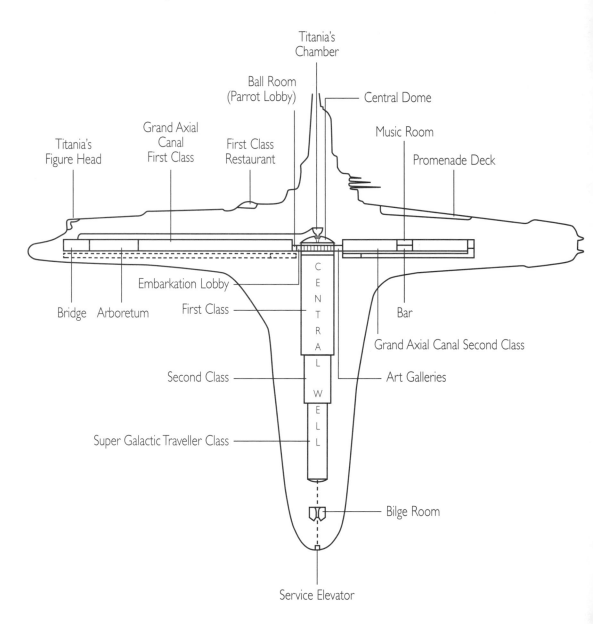

Titania's
Chamber

Ball Room
(Parrot Lobby)

Central Dome

Music Room

Promenade Deck

Grand Axial
Canal
First Class

First Class
Restaurant

Titania's
Figure Head

Embarkation Lobby

Bridge   Arboretum

First Class

Bar

Grand Axial Canal Second Class

Second Class

Art Galleries

Super Galactic Traveller Class

CENTRAL WELL

Bilge Room

Service Elevator

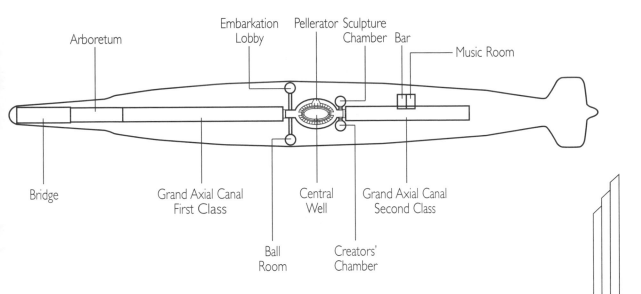

Arboretum

Embarkation Lobby

Pellerator

Sculpture Chamber

Bar

Music Room

Bridge

Grand Axial Canal
First Class

Central
Well

Grand Axial Canal
Second Class

Ball
Room

Creators'
Chamber

STARSHIP TITANIC SPECIFICATION

CLASS: 1a

BEAM: 1.7 enorms

SPAN: 1.3 enorms

SPEED: **Very very fast indeed**

PROPULSION UNIT: **Higgs Old Faithful**

INTELLIGENCE: **Klein und Moebius Gödel**

CREW/PASSENGER RATIO: 1:1

NAV: **Kennigator**

P
L
A
N
S

Been there?
Done that?

Get the 👕.

Voyage deeper into the mystery of the most magnificent Etherliner of all time. Visit the Starship Titanic website at

http://www.starshiptitanic.com

for chat forums, downloadable extras, tech support, an online shop with exclusive Starship Titanic merchandise, holiday ideas, engineering information, Reborzo latest, funny stuff from Michael Bywater, strange pictures by Oscar Chichoni, robot service logs, information about TDV and so on and so on and so on and so on for ever and ever and ever . . . BANG